MW01612492

Lift As You Climb

Public Speakers Inspire and
Communicate Straight From the Heart.

REGAL INNOVATIONS
DENVER, COLORADO

Toastmasters International's trademarks belong to Toastmasters International and are used herein with permission.

Toastmasters International is not affiliated with, does not endorse, nor is promoting this publication.

Regal Innovations
www.itsregal.com

ISBN: 978-0-9827-6803-7

PRINTED IN THE UNITED STATES OF AMERICA

Table of Contents

DEDICATION

This book is dedicated to all of those who have something to say but have been afraid to stand up and say it. Because most of us were once just like you at one time, we pray that you will be inspired to find a local Toastmasters club close to your home or work, and suggest that you take baby steps toward discovering the new you. When you feel that you are scared to death when you are called on to speak in public, we trust that you will use your newfound speaking skills in order to gain a major advantage over others who still fear public speaking.

While being exposed to a wide range of communication experiences, you can join the ranks of more than four million men and women who have benefited from the communication and leadership programs by Toastmasters International, recognized as the world's undisputed expert in public speaking and leadership. Toastmasters International, Inc. currently serves over 260,000 members in 113,000 countries through its 13,800 plus member clubs.

When you say what you say with great passion, body language and voice inflection, you can sometimes touch the soul of a person in ways that were previously impossible. Author and poet Maya Angelou once said "I've learned that people will forget what you said, people will forget what you did, but people will *never* forget how you made them feel." After reading the inspirational writings by our local Toastmasters, we hope that you will recognize that "words are one of the most powerful drugs used by mankind" (Rudyard Kipling), and that you will feel that all of us must challenge ourselves to "lift as we climb." When doing so, you will find that you feel much better about who you are while helping others just like yourself.

ACKNOWLEDGMENTS

We are most grateful to the plethora of Earth angels who were special-sent to help us finish this humane and heartwarming literary project. First, we extend our heartfelt thanks to Mrs. Rosemary Moya (aka "Muddah") who lent her brain and body night after night after night editing, reviewing and re-reviewing our manuscript while being fitted for new glasses. Rosemary, a Denver native, is married and is the mother of one son, three grand children and five great grandchildren. As a great believer in coupons, this woman of love and integrity enjoys the challenge of buying at discount, saving up until she has enough bags to deliver, then giving food to the Friends of the Franciscans, who make two meals per day for the city's street people. Rosemary also gives regularly to the Catholic Community Services, who helps those who receive government assistance. Because God blessed this phenomenal ordinary citizen with a big heart, she has personally cared for many seniors, assisting them in their last years of life as well as remaining by their sides to their final resting ground. Says Rosemary, "I sincerely believe that we will all need help sooner or later, and I will continue to do what I can while I can." Indeed, her seventy-plus years of learning English paid off well for all of us.

At the 13th hour, another dear friend and angel agreed to step up to the plate and offer a final re-review of our entire manuscript. We were so appreciative to Ms. Carol McCartney for her help by providing reassurance and, of course, her polished expertise. Carol, an educator and mother of teen triplets and one high school senior, has taught English for many years and studied post-graduate work in this same field. Indeed we were lucky and blessed to have her come on board and provide her special touch and set of analytical eyes. As a native of the big state of Texas who was transplanted to Georgia, Carol patiently took monumental pride in using her great big red pen to commend and correct each of us. When not reading and writing, Carol can be found working with the Boy Scouts of America, knitting or working on other creative projects - and of course, 24/7 mommy work. Thank you, Carol, for your love and professional touch!

A very special "thank you" goes out to Toastmaster and friend David Bounds, who gallantly agreed to use his time and phenomenal talent to assume the role of our talented and very creative illustrator. Also known as the funniest man in District 26 of Toastmasters International, this good looking, mild mannered artist who hails from the great state of Texas is married to the love of his life, Joanna, and is the father of two children. When he is not hanging out at one of his favorite places in the world, Absolutely Articulate Toastmasters Club or Simply Speaking Toastmaster Club, he can generally be found doodling with his paint brushes and creating another masterpiece.

Mama always said that when one door closes, God will sometimes leave a window cracked for us. For no particular reason, a dear friend and Toastmaster, Carl Thornton amazingly squeezed through our window (during the 13th hour) to offer his last-minute technical assistance to the final page and rear cover of our book.

I will not end without giving honor to God for giving me the ability to lead and share my talent with others. I am also so grateful and appreciative for being blessed with wonderful God-fearing parents (the late James and Elinora Reynolds) who instilled great leadership and entrepreneurial capability in me which has caused me to have great respect and love for others no matter who they are, big or small. By teaching our large family of nine children to always lift as we climb and that no dream is too big, I learned to keep my eyes on the prize and never give up. Indeed this literary book project helped me to remind my children, Roy Shankle and James Funderburke, III, that when we accept a task, we must be true to ourselves and others and finish what we start.

Finally, Elinora, Donna and I are very, very, *very* grateful to each and every person who contributed as a co-author to our first literary book project and for trusting us to start and finally finish what we proposed over a year ago. After all, where else could one go to bring together people from all walks of life and varied experiences in order to bake a cake so tasty that everyone wants a piece of it? Although many thought it would not come to fruition, we all proved that anything is possible when you believe!

Betty Funderburke, DTM, Co-Founder
Absolutely Articulate Toastmasters #1272692

PREFACE

Last year during one of my mentor/mentee meetings with the new, energetic and aspiring President of the Aurorators Toastmasters Club, I mentioned to her that a dear friend of mine, Joe Sabah, once shared this key secret for success with me. Joe said, "If nothing is happening in your life and you seem to be going nowhere, stop complaining and you make the first move to make things happen." Upon sharing this idea with Donna Hilton, we discussed a number of special projects that might put her club on the map. After deciding that the Literary Book Project would be a good one, Donna quickly took her idea back to the Aurorators Toastmasters Club officers, who voted to proceed with this award-winning idea. Looking back in retrospect, I asked myself where else could a group of 50 professionals and their friends and family (in spite of our education and backgrounds) from all walks of life go to instantly become co-authors while becoming rich (in spirit) and famous (even if only in our minds) overnight?

Regarding research to make this good book possible, information was disseminated throughout the year at every major Toastmasters event about our active search for Literary Book Project contributors. In addition, some of us spent many, many more hours via email and finally picking up the phone to call even more prospects to explain our exciting project that promised to make each contributor a co-author. Many expressed that they had been waiting for an opportunity like this for some time! As a result, we ended up attracting members and friends affiliated with over twenty prominent Toastmasters clubs. With 50+ excellent inspirational submissions, we decided that we had enough literary ammunition to rock and roll and move forward. Since our literary project was the first one of its type ever ventured in the Toastmasters District 26 area of Colorado, Wyoming and Nebraska, we had a bit of a bumpy beginning in trying to sell its authenticity and value. However, after sharing that we have a book publisher waiting to be notified of our finished product in order to set us up with the Library of Congress and assign an official ISBN number, many finally realized that we were more than serious. Although we missed the deadline of having our finished product book ready by the time of our 2011 Annual Spring Toastmasters Conference, we still consider our book project a very successful one. During the embryonic stage of this literary project, I acquired more insight and patience than I ever thought I was capable of. Regarding unbroken promises by some who changed their mind about participating at the middle or end of our project, I learned to optimistically smile while staying anchored based on our original concept and dream.

Compiled in alphabetical order, we believe that you will be pleasantly surprised by the sheer genius and creativity expressed in poems and other serious, inspirational and humorous writings (not to mention excellent writing style) by our co-authors in this self-promoting, non-fundraising venture. Based on a strong desire to one day become professional public speakers, our literary book project undoubtedly held a special interest for many serious-minded Toastmasters. Perhaps you will recognize the names of some of our co-authors; they are red-blooded, smart professionals (some famous people) who come from all walks of life and now have a special story to tell. Indeed, these rising stars represent the best of the best of what is good and honorable in our world. I am grateful to these men and women for sharing their experiences and, sometimes, struggles in life in order to make us all stronger and more mature individuals. I once heard that if you keep on doing what you've been doing, you're going to keep on getting what you've been getting. Therefore, if we are fortunate to hear or read a good word from a friend or colleague (no matter their education, age, background or level of experience), it may be possible to alter our lives a bit to improve our course of action. As a matter of fact, I suggest that you get a good cup of international coffee, tea or hot chocolate and get ready for a luxurious, fun ride of your life. And I promise, when you're done reading this book, you will feel more fulfilled, lifted and of course, very inspired.

If it is true that "it is not enough for a person to be good, but they must be good at *something*" (author unknown), we can now testify that we have proven our goodness and worth by sharing inspiring words of hope and encouragement that we hope will tickle your fancy and stimulate you to the core of your heart. Needless to say, we felt that *Lift As You Climb* was the most appropriate title for our challenge to others to stand up, speak out and make a profound difference in a diverse world full of changes, challenges and opportunities.

Elinora Reynolds, DTM, Past President/Co-Founder
Absolutely Articulate Toastmasters #1272692

INTRODUCTION

Sincere thanks to all fellow Toastmasters who took advantage of this momentous opportunity. I also extend special gratitude to Ms. Elinora Reynolds and everyone else who stepped up and contributed time and talent to ensure this literary project was a quality one.

This literary project produced a book of insightful and inspiring messages written by fifty or so brave and creative Toastmasters and friends throughout our district. These pieces are meant to encourage readers to expand their image of themselves and their world and then, in true Toastmasters fashion, share that vision with others. Although most pieces were submitted by fellow Toastmasters in an effort to showcase our organization's talent, we encourage any and everyone to read them.

Some of our authors fearlessly shared their innermost concerns and beliefs in an effort to let others know they empathize with a trying situation, and show what strengthened them through it. Others created captivating written visuals of things that moved them throughout life. All of our authors demonstrated some way in their unique way how Toastmasters has made them evolve and advance with the kind of confidence necessary to live a life where nothing is promised, and many experiences depend solely on one's individual approach to them.

Those of us who collected literary pieces from our fellow Toastmasters were sincerely humbled by the depth and amount of truly gifted members our organization is fortunate to have. It is our pleasure to reward those individuals with a book that will be formally published and have an official ISBN number issued through the Library of Congress. It is a tremendous accomplishment to be a published author. That is something most people dream of but are hesitant to make happen, so a great big *"congratulations"* to those who braved it!

As Toastmasters, we are committed with regard to being proactive about the betterment of ourselves and the world around us. We can be proud that our organization and its members offer the inspiration and means to *"Lift As You Climb."*

Donna Hilton, CC, President
Aurorators Toastmaster Club #2136

FOREWORD

My favorite quote is composed of these two words: "SPEAKERS SPEAK!" And that was true ... until I found a group of speakers who also wrote. Yes, speakers who write and writers who speak, which brings me to introduce you to fifty-three aspiring Toastmasters and friends who joined their talents to bring you this anthology entitled "*Lift As You Climb.*"

As wide-ranged as their speaking talents are, so are their writing skills. You should prepare yourself to laugh at their humor, shed tears when they remind you of real life experiences and smile as you are reminded of truisms that bring you to say, "Ouch, I *knew* that. When am I going to just do it?"

Enjoy! Read, then re-read each story to get the full benefits of these fifty plus courageous Toastmasters and friends who have bonded and banded together in releasing "*Lift As You Climb*" to all the citizens of the world.

Joe Sabah

Joe Sabah is the recipient of the 2009 District 26 Toastmaster Communication & Leadership Award. He is also the founding President of the Colorado Speakers Association, now the National Speakers Association of Colorado.

ANYWAY
Kent M. Keith

People are often unreasonable, illogical and self centered;
Forgive them anyway.

If you are kind, people may accuse you of selfish, ulterior motives;
Be kind anyway.

If you are successful, you will win some false friends and some true enemies;
Succeed anyway.

If you are honest and frank, people may cheat you;
Be honest and frank anyway.

What you spend years building, someone could destroy overnight;
Build anyway.

If you find serenity and happiness, they may be jealous;
Be happy anyway.

The good you do today, people will often forget tomorrow;
Do good anyway.

Give the world the best you have, and it may never be enough;
Give the world the best you've got anyway.

Don't Eat Dung. . .

Imagine that we are all constantly giving and receiving bites of food from and to one another. Some people give wonderful bites of delicious, yummy concoctions: creamy Belgium chocolates, tender pot-roasted beef, juicy watermelon, chewy chocolate chip cookies, crispy cucumbers and fresh, raw almonds. Others give out not so nice bites; day-old French fries, burnt toast, lima beans, moldy Snicker doodles and wilted lettuce. Still others give out disgusting bites: dung. That's right – crap!

Actually, we all give out and receive all three kinds of bites. Now you would think that we would only give and receive the good stuff. But in truth, dung is often in our mouths and hands. Because we like it? Oh No! We hate it! But we often feel we have no choice but to accept it when it is offered to us. And why do we give it out to others? Well, justice for one. We feel they deserve it, or need it. Or we are so full it, that it just pops right out of us.

But our Creator never designed us to eat dung. It is repulsive poison. It never can do us any good. In fact it is quite destructive. It clogs up our system so badly that if we eat enough of it, we will become permanently sick and unable to eat healthy bites. Our whole being will become so polluted by it that even when we try to give out good bites like cantaloupes and crab cakes, they will smell and taste like crap and cow pies. So, here are some "Don't Eat Dung" tips:

1. Make a firm decision to stop eating dung.
2. Learn and discern all the clever ways people serve it up.
3. Just say "No Thanks!" when offered dung. Close your mouth and turn your back.
4. Some people will try to force it on you. You must be firm in not allowing them! Stay away from people like that. And if they throw it on you – throw it right off!
5. The hardest person you will have to resist is, of course, yourself. Ask God to help you every day to stop feeding yourself dung. This will be a big battle but one you can certainly win.

The more you resist dung, the more your body will begin to thrive and heal. You will begin to see just how much cleverly disguised dung *you've* been handing out yourself.

With persistence and time, you will become one of those radiant people overflowing with health, whose generous hands are constantly filled with the best bites of life.

Connie Akins, CC
Simply Speaking Toastmasters #677476
constant_comment@hotmail.com

A Wholistic Approach to Better Health. . .

In my twelve years of practice as a clinical massage therapist, it has come to my attention that many of us do not have a very good idea on how to achieve and maintain better health. Most of the time we wait until our body tells us there is something wrong, usually in the form of pain or discomfort. Unfortunately, this is the wrong approach. Many people come to health care providers and ask them to please help them get better. All we can do is give the necessary service by offering guidelines that may help in avoiding the reason they came in the first place. The following are several suggestions that may be helpful:

1. Exercise: The human body is meant to move. When we don't do any form of exercise, we are doing our body more harm than we can imagine. Something as simple as a fifteen-minute daily walk can help, especially when you swing your arms as you walk. Other kinds of exercise are great to do as well, but remember: moderation is always something to keep in mind.

2. Stretching: If we observe animals, we notice that they instinctively know how important stretching is. Daily stretching helps keep our bodies loose and nimble. Make sure that you warm up before stretching, because without doing so is the same as trying to squeeze a dry sponge.

3. Nutrition and Hydration: I can't overstate how important it is to eat a balanced diet and drink plenty of water. These are the things that fuel our bodies at the cellular level. Without it, we wither away and die. Included in the nutritional aspect is making sure we get the right kind of vitamins and minerals that our body needs. I could go on and on about this particular subject. Most of us (me included) who have what is commonly referred to as "a sweet tooth" are the product of not having the "right" kind of sugars that our bodies need. Research has discovered that we need eight specific kinds of sugars for proper cellular regeneration. The current diet for many of us only addresses two or three of these. Thus, we are constantly craving sweets to satisfy the need our body is craving.

4. Avoid Stress: Stress and tension will not only cause physical harm, but are also a big factor in mental and emotional health. Statistical research confirms this fact. Of course, the best way to deal with stress is to avoid it, if possible. When avoidance is not an option, we must then take a proactive stance by doing things to relieve stress and tension. Driving is one of our daily stressors, for those of us that must do so. I like to give myself more than enough time to get where I am going and if traffic is very heavy, I put on some soothing music.

5. Massage Therapy: This is a subject that I could talk about for days. Massage is not just a "feel good" type of therapy; as a matter of fact, there are dozens of modalities (styles) that can address most things that bother us. For example, Swedish massage is great for circulation and overall relaxation. The Cranial Sacral System is excellent for slowing down the aging process, headaches of all varieties, TMJ, whiplash and neck pain, depression, vision problems, etc. Hand and foot reflexology is also another way that one can gauge what is going on inside our bodies by the tender reflex points that directly relate to some point in our body. Through experience, I have learned that most of these modalities can help in a plethora of ways, especially in helping us to relax and re-energize. It is best to find a good certified massage therapist that has good tactile sense and several different modalities under his/her belt.

6. Sleep: Getting the right amount of sleep (6-8 hours) is extremely important. Our modern-day lifestyle is not only keeping us from getting enough proper rest, but it also robs us of our energy in so many ways that it must be a topic for another article.

Shankara Gil Antero, CC
Absolutely Articulate Toastmasters #1272692
gilito_antero@yahoo.com

Finding Yourself in Toastmasters...

Believe in yourself. Easier said than done, right? Asking yourself, "Well, what does it take?" should be the first question you ask yourself. What are your passions? Dabble around a bit if you must, but figure out what makes you tick. What things do you enjoy and reap the most satisfaction from? For me, making some sort of difference in other peoples' lives was paramount to my feeling influential and recognized. Realizing I wanted to feel influential and recognized was something I discovered while uncovering my passions. What are my passions? Teaching, writing and, though I'd rather swim with sharks on occasion rather than challenge my fear of public speaking, yes, I like public speaking. What a paradox -- to want to influence others and yet to be afraid of your own voice! At the time I joined Toastmasters, I knew I needed to challenge this fear and would need quite a lot of encouragement to do so.

What a wonderful foundation of people that are drawn to a club like Toastmasters. So many people, myself included, need to hear the words to propel us forward in life to overcome our inner challenges. Words like "You are a gifted speaker." (What? What if that is true)? "You have presence when you give a speech." (Really? You mean I'm interesting?) "I really enjoyed hearing your topic and the great job you did to engage your audience." (You liked my speech?!) After about 1003 affirmations (at least!) by my Toastmaster friends, I am finally beginning to believe the words they are saying and that they believe in my abilities...and why shouldn't I? You know that saying your Mom used over and over, "How many times do I have to tell you?" Well, how about "as many times at it takes?" These people see something in me that no one has ever pointed out to me before, and you know what that is? My best self!!! Now I understand why Oprah says "Live your Best Life!" because it truly means "get to know your best self."

Fearful living is the opposite of a fulfilling life because fears are what *you* create in your own mind. The beauty and power of that statement is this: *You* have the power to change your mind about whatever is holding you back. Whew! The four simple words -- "I can do it!" -- are only realized with action, which means bringing your fearful, shaking, sweaty, heart-pounding mind and body to the podium to prove what it can do. That's why self-esteem is *only* built upon accomplishments, rather than hearing compliments and accolades from others. You have something to prove to *yourself* not just receive the accolades bestowed by others. After this, the accomplishment is just icing on your cupcake. Pat yourself on the back and realize the one that counts the most is *you*. So do what you have to do to be your best. You will be so happy that you did. Go hit that proverbial ball right out of the park!

Cybele Antonow
Aurorators Toastmasters #2136
Simply Speaking #677476
cybele750@hotmail.com

Sharecropper's Daughter . . .

While sitting back pondering my rich and interesting life, it occurred to me that God has brought me a mighty long way. Let me tell you about my life.

On September 25, 1954, a bouncing baby girl was blessed to be born to Ben and Pearl Washington on a plantation in Swan Lake, Mississippi; they named her Shirley Jean Washington. I was the seventh of fifteen children; five died at birth. I am so thankful that all ten of us – myself, Dorothy, Ben, Wendell, Jimmie, Deloris, Ladale, Diann, Myertis, Oliver -- *and* both of my parents are still living. Many of my friends are surprised to hear that we were all born at the hands of a midwife, Mrs. Lorraine Baker - the midwife for the plantation that we lived on.

I must say that my parents truly showed their heartfelt love for us and provided for our family as best as they could. Growing up on a plantation, I never felt or even knew that I was poor or lived on a plantation. I only remember my Dad getting up very early every day (before the sun would come up), and not coming back home until the sun was down, working for the plantation owner who paid him very little money because the house we lived in belonged to him. The house that we lived in consisted of four rooms that housed our family of 12; this included a kitchen (with no running water) and three sleeping rooms. We also had an outhouse that we used to go to the bathroom. At night we used a "slop jar" or what others today would call a portable potty. Our baths were taken in a round, #3 metal tub, and of course, because we had no washer or dryer, we washed clothes for our big family of twelve every Saturday using the same #3 tub and a scrub board. Needless to say, because we all worked the Mississippi fields from sun up to sun down seven days a week, we did not have the pleasure of enjoying down time for recreation with friends.

Our lifestyle included manning a *huge* garden for vegetables. Once a year, we killed three to four hogs for meat and lard. After purchasing necessary commodities, my parents had very little left to buy food and clothes for us. While I can honestly say that we *never* went to bed hungry, we learned to be close and love each other with all our heart and soul.

Because my parents were very serious about education, it was mandatory that each of us finish high school *before* we could leave home. Our daily routine included going to the field early in the mornings to pick or chop cotton before going to school. After school, we were required to go back to the fields again. My parents wanted the very best for us in life, so by the grace of God, we all finished high school. While one sibling decided to join the military, others went on to further their education via the college route. Today, I am happy to say that our immediate family is *blessed* to consist of two doctors, one lawyer, some politicians and many, many teachers.

My dad was blessed to make it to the 8th grade before his education abruptly ended, and Mama had a tenth grade education. When I entered the seventh grade, both parents chose to go back to school since my dad always had a desire to sign his name in cursive. Based on continuation of his education, we were very proud of daddy when he finally learned how to sign his name! Meanwhile, my mom was *blessed* to become the lead teacher in a local Head Start program where she worked for 30 years. Destined to lead by example, *determination* and *perseverance* have been my parents' keys to success by encouraging each of us to always do our very best.

I remember the day that my Dad finally got the courage to put in an application to work at the Mississippi State Penitentiary. For references, the State called Mr. Mike, the owner of our plantation. However, because my father was considered the best tractor driver on the plantation, Mr. Mike gave an unsatisfactory reference and refused to let my dad go to work elsewhere. Truly, I had never seen my father so hurt and disappointed. As a result of this experience, my father swore that he would *never* again let another man have that much control over his destiny. After saving his money for what seemed like a lifetime, my dad finally saved enough money to purchase a small two bedroom home (office of civil rights leader, Fannie Lou Hamer's[1] home) in Ruleville, Mississippi.

---

[1] Mrs. Fannie Lou Hamer (1917-1977) was a leader in the civil rights movement during the 60's and 70's. As a pioneer in the voting rights struggle in Mississippi, Ms. Hamer was severely beaten by the police and later testified before the Democratic National Convention in 1964. She was the vice-chair of the Mississippi Freedom Democratic Party. In 1962 (without her knowledge or consent) she was sterilized by a doctor as a part of the state of Mississippi's plan to reduce the number of poor people in the state. In 1963, after being

Later Dad reapplied for employment at the State Penitentiary and was finally hired as a driver. Because my Dad was sick and tired of going to work clean and coming back home dirty every day, he was finally blessed to have a job that he could go to work clean and neat everyday (in starched uniform and ironed-creased pants with boots shining), and come home clean and happy – just what he always wanted. Now, Dad worked only five days per week, eight hours per day *and* he even received paid holidays. He was *blessed* to work at the State Penitentiary until he retired at age 70.

Because we were taught that our outside appearance reflects on how you feel on the inside, my parents emphasized taking care of ourselves and told us "if you look good, you will also perform good ... and feel good about yourself." At an early age, we were taught to take pride in ourselves and to treat others as we wanted to be treated.

While God has blessed me by allowing me to grow older with a family of my own (five college-educated children and eight grandchildren), I realize that being a

---

charged with disorderly conduct, Hamer was beaten so badly in jail, that she was permanently disabled. She lectured extensively, and was known for a signature line she often used - "I'm sick and tired of being sick and tired." She was known as a powerful speaker, and her singing voice lent another power to civil rights meetings in the south. Ms. Hamer brought a Head Start program to her local community in Mississippi, and later founded the Freedom Farm Cooperative in 1969. She also helped found the National Women's Political Caucus in 1971. In 1972, the Mississippi House of Representatives passed a resolution honoring her national and state activism Suffering from breast cancer, diabetes, and heart problems, Fannie Lou Hamer died in Mississippi in 1977.

11

sharecropper's daughter wasn't so bad after all – especially when you're surrounded with an abundance of love and happiness. Truly, if we could have had all the money in the world, we couldn't have been any happier as a family!

Of the many things that I learned from the patriarch of my rich, beloved family, two key facts are that nobody can hold you down and we *must* always put God first. As I sit here pondering over my rich and interesting life, I realize that, without a shadow of a doubt, the Lord has brought me a mighty long way.

Shirley Armstrong
Absolutely Articulate Toastmasters #1272692
SArmstrong54@msn.com

The Lord Works in Mysterious Ways. . . .

The following is a personal letter written to some of our friends by my late husband, Joe, and me when we were traveling doing missionary work in Eastern Europe. From 1984 through 1992, we were blessed to travel to Romania, Czechoslovakia, Poland, Russia and Hungary doing missionary work. My husband and I parented six biological children (Stan, Steve, Kathy, Joyce, Robert and Nancy) as well as about ten foster children. During my husband's 84 years of life, we traveled extensively and learned so much from our extended family as well as all of those we were blessed to meet along the way. As an 83-year-old widow (of two years), I hope that you will enjoy one of the letters from our travels that will reflect a glimpse of the rich life that Joe and I had together as devoted missionaries. This letter was written in 2004, during a return trip to Romania, Hungary and Czechoslovakia.

Dear Friend:

We want to share with you the story of our adventures of being on our own in Romania after our director, Hank, and the tour group left us behind (at our request). We told the director that we wanted to spend more time with some long ago friends.

We traveled by shuttle from Timisoara, Romania to the Budapest Airport – a big difference from the old days.

From there, we went on to the train station but we arrived two hours late due to tire problems on the van. This meant we had missed the afternoon international train. What to do – find a room nearby and return to the station tomorrow or take the late train and arrive in Slovakia at 11:00 PM. Unfortunately, the friends we wanted to see had both moved, and we did not have their new addresses or phone numbers. Although we had sent an email, we were not certain that there would be someone there to meet us. We decided to go on, and berated ourselves most of the way for making such a stupid mistake.

We had no Slovakian money, no ATM machine, the International ticket office was closed, the money exchange was closed and the only store open refused to change money for us, even for a phone call. When talking to the taxi driver outside, he refused to change our money or take us anywhere. Walking back inside, this disreputable looking old lady with clothes all tattered and torn approached me. Her clothes were all safety-pinned together – certainly not the kind of person one would want to trust, and we had been trying to avoid her. Looking back at what happened, I think that God was trying to teach us a lesson here. This lady got my attention when she asked if I could speak Deutsch (German). I said, "a little." Amazingly, she began to tell me what to do. Every time I lapsed back into English, she screamed at me, "*SPRECH DEUTSCH!*" Meanwhile another character had been following us around - just the kind you are warned about in train stations. He looked like an old hippie (a bleary-eyed one) but he could speak some English and some Deutsch. Now we had a three-way conversation.

This old lady told me to convince a cab driver to take us to the Hotel Slovan, a very nice hotel, but "teur" (expensive), so don't plan to stay there; however, they would exchange money for us. After you have money to pay the driver, she suggested that we have the taxi driver take us to a "pension," a cheaper place to stay.

Meanwhile, a young cab driver who stood nearby and had listened to our whole conversation, agreed to take us. Putting our lives in his hands, we cautiously went with him. Hotel Slovan was a beautiful 4-star hotel and they took Visa. I decided to take a room there -- after all by now, it was five minutes 'til midnight. I hoped for about $80 but when we heard it was over $100, we decided to do it anyway; but we hadn't counted on what our cab driver did. He came in after us and even though we couldn't understand his language, we KNEW what he was saying! He told the clerk, "these people do not have much money, and they can't afford your hotel; they need something cheaper." Turning directly to me, he asked, "Do you want a cheaper hotel?" "Well," I responded to the clerk, "Yours is a little expensive." "Okay, I will tell you what to do. Have the driver take you to the Hotel Academia; you can trust him. It is a nice, clean hotel and will only cost you about $35 a night." He was right. It was a nice, clean hotel and the price range was $23 - $45, depending on the type of suite. We learned later that it is a training hotel for young people to learn the hotel and restaurant trade. We thanked God for a safe haven for the night.

The next morning, we told God that we still needed help finding our friends. Before going down to the lovely buffet breakfast included with our room, we read Psalm 121 – "The Lord watches over your comings and goings..."

We chose a table in the center of the room, even though there were many others available. We could overhear a nearby conversation. Going over to the two men talking together, I said, "I hear American voices and you were talking about church." "Yes," resounded this big booming voice. "I'm Dick Larson from a Medical Mission, and who are you?" I told him, and he asked "What are you doing in Slovakia?" I responded by telling him that we have a problem. "We are here to visit friends but they have moved and through a series of mishaps, we do not have the new addresses or phone numbers." He asked what their names were; although he didn't know the first one, he laughed when I mentioned the second name. We were shocked when Dick said, "We were in their home last night; our interpreter will be here in ten minutes and he will have their phone number."

When we called, my friend of many years ago said, "I was hoping to hear from you today, and that you would be here as something has come up and this is the only day that we can spend with you." Yes, we were meant to go the day before and it was clear that this was the place that we were intended to stay. Once again, we received confirmation that the Lord works in mysterious ways. It may not be our timing, but it is definitely His!

Later, we returned to the station to look for "our angels" just to say thank you, but could not find any of them. There is so much more that we could share about our exciting time in Slovakia and Hungary, but we won't bore you with what. To us, these were very interesting moments. Perhaps when we see each other again, we can share the rest of our amazing story about our travels in Europe. God bless you, my friends.

Best regards,
Joe and Alice Austin

Alice Austin
Absolutely Articulate Toastmasters #1272692
smaustin@q.com

Kid Again. . .

Do you have those friends that bring out the kid in you? Yeah, you heard it correct: The kid in you? Are you in your 20's, 30's, 40's, 50's, 60's, 70's, 80's, 90's, 100's and look at the younger age people and call them kids? So if you are 65, you look at the 50 year olds as *kids*? What if you are 65 and look at the 70 year olds as "kids"? We should all strive to be kids at every age. How do we maintain our "kidhood" through "adulthood"?

Friends, recently I went snowshoeing with a friend of mine that I haven't seen in one or two months. Do you have friends that you can just pick up where you left off - even if it has been weeks, months or maybe even years? Young children can pick where they left off so why shouldn't we? I've always strived to have friends that can handle waiting a bit to reconnect due to the busyness of being an adult! Well, now to snowshoeing. My friend is fun; she is a kid at heart. Both of us are in our 30's. We haven't snowshoed together for a year. One of her 'kid at heart' friends told her how she goes snowshoeing with a sled. So my friend brought a nice lightweight, red plastic sled. We snowshoed up a mountain and then decided to utilize the red sled. We hopped on with her taking the lead and holding her snowshoes, while I held on to my gear, and off we went!

Neither of us had gone sledding for years. Why not? "Adulthood." What changes? Age. In all the 15 years that I have been snowshoeing, I've never used a sled. Why was I open to using a sled this time? Though I am aging, I realized that I'm still a *kid at heart*.

While choosing to be open to *something new*, I also enjoy surrounding myself with friends who share the same kind of heart and openness. It occurred to me that in spite of my kid at heart outlook on life, I also get wrapped up in the burdens (and expectations) of adulthood. Needless to say, this makes for a constant tug-o-war between "kidhood" and "adulthood."

Regarding this tug-o-war seeming battle surrounding age, the truth of the matter is that my heart and soul desires to be young and free. I am so grateful for my snowshoeing buddy and the rest of my 'kid at heart' friends. Why? Because I realize that getting older each year doesn't mean that I can't act (and do) spontaneous, fun things like kids sometimes do.

Are you and your friends "kids at heart" who could appreciate moments of being a kid again? If not, I highly recommend it!

Neisha Balleck
Simply Speaking Toastmasters #677476
balleck@gmail.com

Collisions with Destiny . . .

It seems if there is justice in life, behind every nightmare there has to be an amazing dream awaiting its cue to flourish. I remember times when a relationship went sour, and I would ask God to intercede; I asked for a miracle, promising to do all that was in my power to make the relationship work. That is not the way life goes. It takes at least two to form a relationship, be it a love, business or a wonderful friendship.

Initially, I made a choice (persuaded by social customs and involving sacrifices) to marry and have children. This meant an end to a college education; I was a wife and soon afterwards, a mother. I loved having a family; however, life continued to evolve within the structure of my world. The time had come when my circle of life took on different shapes. Friends married, divorced, moved, etcetera. A friendship of more than forty years dissolved at the blink of an eye when I made a conscious decision to fulfill some of the dreams I had put on hold over the years. After raising the children, I went back to school. My friend, Starlet, said I no longer fit in her world. She decreed I was too "highfalutin" for her, and she had no desire to continue our friendship. Her words created a nightmare within my soul.

Losing my dear friend was difficult, but freeing myself was a blessing beyond belief. We were no longer anchored by each other's approval. Our bond of friendship collided with destiny for the sake of both our human potentials. We needed to free each other to follow our individual paths. I went on to realize my dream of becoming a psychologist, and she went on to search for her reality. I thank God for the past, present and future.

Carolyn Betts
FACCMasters Toastmasters #5086
carolynbetts@comcast.net

EnvironMental . . .

*Believe in yourself. Easier said than done, right? Regarding humor, there's a saying that goes, "Death is easy - Comedy is hard!" I don't know who it's attributed to (probably Dr. Kevorkian), but it's false. Comedy is pretty easy. Just remember what makes you laugh, and try to pass it on to others. I hope you enjoy the excerpt from one of my 5-7 minute speeches, as well as this book. It's got Toastmaster humor, insight, feelings and attitude. And **that's** just the cover!*

David Bounds

As I was walking into my house the other day, I discovered a piece of candy in my pocket. It was a Hershey's Kiss, and I love those things. So I unwrap it, pop it into my mouth and as I'm rolling that little piece of foil into a little ball, I spot the trashcan way across the room. And I say to myself, "why should I walk all the way over the room to throw it away when I can instead pretend …that I'm in the biggest basketball game of my life!"

It's game seven of the NBA finals! My team is down by two points, and there's only two seconds left on the clock! I look over to my coach and ask, "Coach, please! Can I take the last shot?"
And he says, "Yeah...in your dreams!"

So I say, "Well, *this is* my dream, Coach, so thanks!"

Just then, out of the corner of my eye, I see perhaps the greatest defender of the trash basket of all time - my wife, Joanna, and she's racing across the floor to guard me. I hurry up and take the in-bounds pass but, she forces me to change my shot at the last second... from my patented three point, fall-away jumper, to my very unpatented, run away, no-look, over-the-back prayer shot. And as I turn around, I see her jump up and KA-PII-YA! She slaps it to the ground. Game over! Dinner served! And as she hits the floor, she's saying "Don't you dare throw anything away that can be recycled in this house! This is my house!"

And it occurred to me that maybe that's the first time I've heard that sports expression where it was actually true.

She continued . . . "Haven't I told you about the three R's - Reduce, Reuse, and Recycle?"

"Well yeah! But maybe there should be a fourth 'R' - maybe it should be Reduce, Reuse, Recycle and REALLY?" I mean REALLY? "Joanna, it was just a little piece of aluminum foil!"

I said to myself, "David, the Hershey's Company Worldwide makes over 30 MILLION of those little kisses a DAY! And if you took all the wrappers off of all those kisses, flatten them all out and put them all back together, you know what you'd have?"

"I don't know... calluses?" I answered.

The truth of the matter is you would have about 133 square miles of aluminum foil - ALL of which usually ends up in a landfill EVERY DAY! "And you're telling me, Joanna, that you're willing to trash this entire planet over a little piece of chocolate?"

"Well....," I said, "There was an almond in there, too."

And at this point I'm I thinking ". . . man!" Sometimes Joanna can really put the "MENTAL" in Environmental!

Why is she going on about those three R's to me anyway? I do them!

I REDUCE! I save electricity. She wanted me to go out and get a paper shredder for our home office, but you know what I did instead? I went to the local animal shelter and bought us a puppy! Now that's an old school paper shredder! Furthermore, I think I save more energy than anyone I know. Some of my friends carpool to work and some of them bike to work. Well, to save energy, I don't even go to work!

I REUSE! See this plastic sandwich bag? Circa 1965! I even go around the house trying to think of new items to reuse. Things that people don't normally think about - I think I've come up with a good one. You know, there's nothing we like more around the holidays than to entertain.
    And this year, nothing is going to say Christmas around our household any better than these little miniature yule log party poppers. And see what they're made of? Empty toilet paper rolls! "Won't Joanna be pleased?"

And I RECYCLE! Heck, I've already recycled two or three jokes in this speech already. And I put all my papers in one bin, cans in another bin and glass in the other bin. And then I just wrap up everything else and throw it in my kids' rooms. They don't mind; after all, they're teenagers. Their rooms always look like landfills every day of the week! But that's just until Joanna can help me sort it out. And I do need help.

Look, deep down, I know Joanna's right. She has a real passion for this planet, and it's one of the things I love about her. I even told her so. I had it engraved on that wood chipper I bought her on our anniversary. And so now I'm happy to say that we're on the same team working those three R's together. And I even do the fourth one. Because I really, I mean really try to understand her environmental concerns. And in return, I am happy to say that she's finally starting to show me the respect I deserve. I know because whenever I tell her I've come up with a new environmental idea, she will say to me, "Well, let's hear it Einstein!" And that guy was, like really smart…right?

So, just for the record: I've got to tell you that I have officially retired from trash ball. I have more important things to think about... like the environment. But every now and again, I will still sneak out for a little pick-up game. It's just a different kind of "pick-up game" now.

David Bounds
Absolutely Articulate Toastmasters #1272692
Simply Speaking #677476
dbounds607@gmail.com

Gifts . . .

They come in all size and packages. Sometimes the gifts that are poorly wrapped have the most meaning. The old saying, "you can't judge a book by its cover" also hold true with gifts. I reflect back on times in my last marriage when Christmas was a big formal event. The months leading up to the day of celebration were overwhelming. What did I want, and what were their expectations? The motives behind the gift-buying were about impressing the receiver. How do I measure up, and was I going to be judged by the gift that was offered? It was a time where what we gave was more important and meaningful than the intent. On Christmas morning, we all went over to the "in-laws" house to see a living room full of gifts. There were at least 30 gifts per person. The entire living room was filled with neatly wrapped gifts, all color coordinated with matching ribbons and bows. To reflect upon my childhood, the money my in-laws spent on the external wrappings were worth more than the gifts I ever received as a child.

Growing up as the child of an alcoholic single mother, we learned that our needs were not important. There were years that we would not have had a Christmas had it not been for our grandmother. After I grew up, I learned that my grandmother was a very critical and judgmental person. This is probably one of the factors leading to my mother's unhappiness, which led her to "self-medicate" with alcohol to cope with raising five children alone. But as children, grandmother was our hero and was able to create the magic of Christmas. Instead of fear of abandonment and strange men in and out of the house where we lived, we had the security of a tree and a few gifts under the tree. She had provided us with the gift of security. There was also a regimen of predictability that Santa would deliver the goods. If it was only a doll and a stuffed animal, it was a doll of love and a stuffed animal that had the large floppy ears that would listen to your fears and worries. My grandmother was able to provide the security of a perfect tree because there was unconditional love. There were stockings hung over the fireplace that had every one of our names written on them - Kim, Jody, Megan, Marcy and Bill. We had names that someone had spent time using Elmer's glue and some nice sparkly glitter to let us know that we mattered and were loved. These gifts might seem so insignificant to some people, but they meant the world to me. When I opened the presents, I felt that someone took the time to give me something because they thought how important it was to give me a gift. The gift that was given was the gift of hope.

I often wonder if my grandmother understood how crucially important these gifts were. As an adult, I now understand that she tried to make up for what my mother was unable to give because she was a very sick woman. Truly, she only cared about herself and feeding her addiction to alcohol. Realistically, she was incapable of giving love to her children. As for me, I, unfortunately, spent most of my life taking my family's hardships personally by thinking that I was a bad person and was the primary reason for my dad's departure.

Before my father died, I realized he had his own demons and retracted into self absorbed, narcissistic, obsessive-compulsive routines. He (just like my mother) was both unable to give or receive love. After investing many hours in a group counseling session conversing with 12 strangers who were raised in similar family environments, the realization that I was not at fault was one of the best gifts that I could have ever received.

I now know that I am fully capable of giving love but -- most importantly -- I deserve to receive love. This spiritual awakening has changed my life, and today I am able to apply the principles of giving *and* receiving loving gifts. Every Christmas, I buy the most beautiful, bright eyed doll baby with beautiful hair, and donate it to a needy child hoping that a needy and worthy little girl will feel the gift of hope just as I felt from my grandmother. In an effort to instill within my daughter the importance of giving, every year I would bring her shopping to help me pick out such a special doll. The purpose of this exercise was to help her understand that it's not about the external gifts with the fancy wrapping to impress others that are important. Instead, it is heartfelt kindness and gifts from the heart (no matter the cost) that really matter.

After my marriage dissolved, it was difficult for me to even celebrate Christmas. I gave away my artificial pine tree and all the ornaments that I had collected over the years. The pressures of the holidays were soon a thing of the past, and I found a simpler way to celebrate holidays. I am now in a relationship with a very loving and humbled man, who also struggled with the pretense of pretentious gift giving. We have agreed to give the gift of love – kind words, service and generosity. Last year for Christmas, the gifts we exchanged were homemade. He made a cutting board out of the scrap wood from the hardwood floors that I had installed in my house. He told me that if I should ever move from my house, I will always have a piece of my old home with me. As for me, I made a lovely, hand-painted piece for him made from items taken from his ranch.

At long last, I have finally learned that gifts are best given when they are given from the heart.

Marcy Brack
Simply Speaking Toastmasters #677476
mbrack827@msn.com

Stars . . .

A little boy showed me that being quiet isn't always an option. His sister taught me to appreciate silence while it lasted.

She and I used to lie in the grass at midnight, wrapped up in blankets and staring at the blackest of blue skies. Sometimes we would talk; but often, we just relished in the nature around us. From where we lay, under the oak tree in her backyard, we could hear the crickets' orchestra being accompanied by undertones of the wind and an excerpt from the owls. It was a symphony performed just for the two of us.

On a quiet night in late April, we talked. The symphony must have been booked for another location because we could not hear anything but ourselves. Either that, or we were laying on the conductor.

I was in the middle of a story that's been lost to the years, and she obviously wasn't paying attention. All of the sudden, she hushes me and points up.

A thought fell off her lips.

"Emma, if you're really silent, you can hear the stars talking to each other."

Emma Bretz (age 13)
Daughter of Cherry Creek Toastmasters Member #2977
joan@bretztec.com

The Universal Language . . .

> *"A musician must make music;*
> *an artist must paint;*
> *a poet must write;*
> *-if he is to ultimately be at*
> *peace with himself."*
> Abraham Maslow

My name is Lee E. Brown, Jr., and as a professional saxophonist and educator who have lived in the beautiful rocky mountain region of Colorado for over thirty years, I would like to share my thoughts about the importance of music. Born and raised in Kansas City, Missouri (nicknamed "The Paris of the Plains") and notorious home of a unique style of jazz and home to big-name music stars like Count Basie, Charlie Parker, Joe Turner, Ben Webster, William Page and many others, my father, Lee E. Brown, Sr. (also a professional saxophonist) inundated our family with the sweet, melodic sounds of soulful music. In the music arena, I have worked as a conductor in the public school environment, and recorded with some of the city's best musicians while performing with a plethora of accomplished musicians in a variety of genres including rhythm and blues, soul, traditional and contemporary jazz and funk. In Kansas City, I performed with the Inner City Orchestra and was later privileged to join a team of local musicians who participated in a New Orleans Katrina project recorded by Home Box Office (HBO). As a professional musician and connoisseur of good music, I can attest that music is my life, my passion and the force that drives me to excellence. In essence, it is who I am and what I do.

Music is life, commitment, work, discipline, fun, sorrowful, joyful - and all things in one. As I see it, music is the beat, the rhythm and the sound of life. When many of us hear music, we experience a wide spectrum of emotions that makes us smile, love and even cry. But from the beginning of time, our emotions have been expressed through music. Many believe that music is *the personality of life* which defines the mood and character of whoever is writing or performing. Because music cannot be expressed in words, it is considered the "universal language" that expresses all emotions. As poetry is for the ear and soul, music represents freedom and serves as an effective tool to unwind and de-stress. Defined by dictionary.com as "an art of sound in time that expresses ideas and emotions in significant forms through the elements of rhythm, melody, harmony and color," music is one thing that is important to almost every society. Having been around for almost as long as modern man, the tapping of one's foot, humming, or any sweet, pleasing or harmonious sound is an excellent example of how music moves us.

Based on my extensive training, I believe that music can be characterized by certain qualities such as pitch, melody, rhythm and frequency. Consequently, each type of music is characteristic by certain degrees of these qualities. For example, a rhythmic music characterizes joy while a melody expresses romance. Again, a melody also expresses sorrow. If we look back to Western Classical, it connects us to something universal about human emotions, and it makes us reach a transcendental stage of mind. One of the notable composers of Western Classical music was Ludwig Van Beethoven, who gifted the world with musical masterpieces despite of being paralyzed with deafness at a very young age of twenty-eight.

Music is art, calming food and fuel for the soul. As the ultimate expression of deep human emotion, it is the embodiment of human emotions put in the most tangible form possible to evoke the emotions in others. It can persuade, influence and inspire the young and the old and can take you to new or imaginary places while making you feel good. Music is life; without it, there would be no individuality or spirit of creativity. Music is a universal language, and is an adventure, love, anger, passion, life, language, love and so much more. As an expression of human emotions, music expresses joy, ecstasy, romance, and also sorrows, pathos and agony. In the words of P.B. Shelly, "Our sweetest songs are those which tell our saddest thoughts." Surprisingly, a simple song which is sung from the heart gives us more pleasure than a complex one which is often influenced by human artifacts.

There are many different kinds of music, all with different feels such as jazz, rock, classical, country, folk, western, bluegrass, reggae, techno, rap and so on. Although they are different, they are united under the same definition of music. Music is a universal (international) language that connects people to one another without words. It is a medium of expression that cannot be felt or seen, but affects and connects us at the deepest level; because music is life, it is you, me and everything around all of us. It even encompasses every sound we make and every step we take … and every thought that goes though our mind. No matter what action we take, music is involved in some way. Since music is a universal language that transcends nationality, race, creed - even time itself - it connects people together and brings the past, present and future into the hearts and minds of everyone. As a result, it is everything to everyone – even to those who don't understand it. If you can imagine a world without music, you will see absolutely nothing at all because in one way or another, everything makes music.

Next to the word of God, music deserves the highest praise. When praying and playing music, I feel closest to God. As a matter of fact, I believe that music is God's gift to us which gently touches us in a way that is special and unique. Representing the heart, mind and soul, music is the essence of all life and absorbs the soul by releasing passion. Without life, we wouldn't have music, and without music, there would be no life. Because music is life, love, ecstasy, creativity, joy, laughter, excitement, inspiration, prosperity, happiness, pain, sorrow, anger, emotion and everything good, it gives us a voice to change the world, and it is the magic that keeps the world believing even when our faith falters. While offering us a way to ultimately relax, music gracefully allows us to connect with all people and connects us to the past, comforts us in the present and offers us hope for the future.

Throughout the world, in the biggest and smallest regions, music is one of the most appreciated gifts that can be found. As one of the only ways to communicate with the stars, it can make you feel (without the aid of drugs) like you are capable of doing whatever you want and wherever you want to do it. Since this universal language allows us to express what we cannot express in words – like powerful medicine that stops time - it is capable of making us forget everything we're doing at this moment and can take us back to a special memory. For me, music is my pulse, and without it, my world would be a very sad and different place – as it would be for others.

Lee E. Brown, Jr.
Friend of Absolutely Articulate Toastmasters #1272692
leebo1795@comcast.net

Guess Who? . . .

As a child, I was encouraged to read and learn as much as I could, as often as I could.

I wrote letters to everyone I knew including men and women in the Armed Forces and relatives and friends too.

As a proud member of the Children's Choir and later the Men's Choir of my church, I never imagined that I would one day do some acting as an adult.

What a difference a day makes!

Because I want to leave a lasting touch on everyone that I meet, I have taught and mentored many in my profession as a teacher and a father.

So who do I give credit to for my life's accomplishments? God – the Ultimate Teacher and Author!

Leroy Brown
Absolutely Articulate Toastmasters #1272692
TheEduCtr@aol.com

You Are Loved . . .

I grew up being told that I was a mistake because my parents had not planned on a fifth child. Additionally, all of us children were constantly reminded we had to be perfect in every way - perfectly groomed, perfectly thin with a perfect look like fashion models or movie stars. I remember my mother giving me a look (accompanied by a hateful voice) when she would say, "Look at you ... you're a disgrace!" She added, "Maybe you won't be so bad once you get rid of all that baby fat!" And, of course, my only brother would sneer at me while saying with disgust, "Glasses, braces... you're all messed up!"

Throughout my grade school years, I had one pseudo friend who reminded me on a daily basis how awful I was. In a matter-of-fact tone, she would always say to me, "You're so ugly and you'll still be ugly when you grow up; no one will ever marry you!" I tolerated her torment for years because it was either that or spend the dreaded recesses and lunchtime all alone. Because of my desperation for acceptance, I endured this special friendship.

When coming home from school, my sisters and I would hope that our mother was in a good mood. If she was, we were safe for the time being. If she wasn't, that was a different story. You see, it was not uncommon for Mom to have fits of anger for no apparent reason. Although she never gave an explanation for our wrong-doing, the worse we "misbehaved," the more severe the punishment.

Because my oldest sister and I were deemed the "ugly ones," we bore the brunt of the abuse.

Since violent behavior was familiar to me, I was not surprised when my first husband treated me the same way. He frequently took his frustrations out by using me as a punching bag. When I tried to get away, he would grab hold of my hair, making it impossible to escape. As I tried to compose myself after these horrible incidents, I smoothed my hair while discovering long black strands that had come loose in my hand. What a life! This is when I finally realized that I was a human being and did not deserve the abuse — nor to be treated as an inanimate object, much like a rag doll that has been torn asunder.

Having lost the will to live, God only knows how I survived all of the years of mistreatment. I do know that throughout my whole life, God has loved me. He has given me the strength to continue to face each day with a hopeful attitude for a better future. Thankfully, years later I have been blessed with a life full of happiness and unconditional love from the many wonderful people I have met — especially from my current husband, Hugh.

Friends, always remember that no matter how others may have mistreated you, it is *not* because of you, but because of the problem(s) your abuser has. Also know that you are loved just for being wonderful you.

Gina Curley, DTM
Night Speakers Toastmasters #810454
Gina.Curley@indra.com

You are Infinite . . .

Your life is based on the amount of energy inside, not outside, of you. Once ego and limit are lost, you, in turn, become infinite, kind and beautiful. Imagine the possibilities, and imagine the experience!

Growing up, I was reminded over and over again that I could be whoever I wanted to be and that I could also do whatever I wanted to. This means anything at all once you put your mind to it and work hard toward that goal! Today, I run with those powerful words of advice. In spite of the fact that I sometimes experience difficulty conveying these words of wisdom with to own children, I tell them that they must try to do the right thing in life and not be afraid to try everything that they are passionate about. I also encourage them to always speak up for what they desire because, as my Mom always said, "a closed mouth will never get fed." Over the years, I discovered that I am limitless and courageous while unafraid to try anything once. I have and will continue to do so – and so can you!

In May 2010 when I entered the Mrs. Colorado Pageant, I was given the key to unlock the door to personal excellence. After having time to reflect on my experience, I finally understood that due to limitless boundaries in time and space, I am privy to infinite possibilities to achieve greater things, whether that time is now or in the future. No matter what the outcome may be, I promised myself that I would try and try, again and again!

Be brave; use your courage to take a step towards greatness because *sometimes* this is a gift that only some of us have. Broaden your horizons and live your dream; never let a neglected opportunity stand in your way. "Why?" you may ask. Because this is something you can never retrieve!

Sherise Frank
Absolutely Articulate Toastmasters #1272692
Sfrank1903@earthlink.net

The Calling . . .

As a young girl, I remember there was an older couple in the neighborhood where I grew up, the Colemans. Mr. Coleman was a tall, stout man and his wife was rather short and petite. Mr. Coleman was the usual neighborhood watchman, and he knew everything that went on in our area. Of course, he would not hesitate (as a matter of fact, he seemed to enjoy) letting our parents know when he saw us children doing something wrong.

He was also a generous man and had a house filled with all kinds of goodies. Mr. Coleman was also very active in his church and because Mrs. Coleman's health had changed, he asked my mother if I could stay and look out for her. As I look back today and review significant glimpses of my childhood, I realize that it was an honor and privilege to care for Mrs. Coleman. I'll never know if Mr. Coleman saw the calling in me at an early age or if it was merely a coincidence.

Going through high school, I, like many teens, got a job. One of the jobs where I happened to be hired was working in a convalescent home. What a great honor and a privilege to care for the elderly!

After leaving high school, I worked for over five years in the banking industry. Due to God's calling, I eventually returned to the call of caring for elderly and disabled individuals. This passion continued to grow fast and deep as I began to know who God was in my life. In order to cater to this special class of people, He specifically gave me instructions on how to start my own business.

Being the only girl, my mother and I had a special bond, so I shared with her the command given to me by our Heavenly Father. She was as excited as I was and was eager to do what she could to help me as only a Mother could for her child. She worked diligently by my side with our first client and then with many others. Who would know that, eleven years later, this special lady would require the same care she so freely gave to others? Due to the knowledge and grace of helping others, this experience equipped me to serve my dear Mother, though it was sometimes challenging. Indeed, it has been an honor and a privilege to care for my idol and earth angel – my Mother. More than anything, I am forever grateful that I have been able to keep her in our home for almost a decade. I am also grateful to God for the wonderful caregivers that He has placed in my life over the years in order to make my mother's round-the-clock care possible. Finally, twenty six years later, I also owe a great amount of gratitude to my professional team of dedicated, outstanding caregivers who have made this agency what it is today.

Now I realize that every one of us in life has a call and a purpose. I encourage you to seek out your calling and purpose so that you can effectively proceed through this life without doubt or question.

Renee Franklin
Absolutely Articulate Toastmasters #1272692
expertnursingservice@yahoo.com

The Ultimate Gift. . .

What if you woke up one morning and reached down to scratch your leg, but couldn't feel anything? Would you panic and cry out as you discovered that you were paralyzed from your waist down? What if your service pet, that you had spent the last 5 years of your life with since becoming handicapped, suddenly passed away? How would you make it when it appeared that your dog helped you with essential duties like opening and closing doors, turning on lights, helping you cross the street and even helping you put your clothes and shoes on? Would you give up and declare that you had lost your only friend? What if you were given the pink slip from your job of 35 years after being replaced with a younger college graduate that you had to train? Would you go "postal" or look for the first bridge to take a leap?

What if your spouse, after 40 years of marriage, decided to replace you by regressing back to date a younger person? Would you kick your significant other to the curb, sink into a deep depression or want to get rid of the competition? What if you went to bed and woke up the next morning only to discover someone in the mirror who resembled you but was a different color? Would you freak out and refuse to go to work with a desire to run and hide? Or would you see history repeat itself as you girded up your loins with all the things that experience had taught you about treating all people with love and respect? What if in the religious persuasion you had chosen, the parishioners turned against you and denied knowing you - such as the disciples did to Jesus? Could you in good conscience continue to respond to them in kindness anyway?

What if you and your best friend from elementary school were wed and spent 30 years together only to find out that he/she was dying and only had a short time to live? Would you remember your vows "till death do you part" or would you begin to immediately search for a replacement to live the duration of your life with? What if your family lost all respect for you because you spent a little time away behind locked bars for a crime you contended you were innocent of? Would you forgive them anyway for not giving you the benefit of the doubt and viewing you with love and fairness? Or would you retaliate with the same vengeance they directed toward you?

Toastmasters and friends, did you know that in spite of all of the "what ifs" in our life, we still have the right to claim the ultimate gift, called "hope"? You don't have to buy it since it doesn't cost anything; high intellect or special credentials are not prerequisites to qualify for it. As long as you have hope, you will always have the key to the ultimate gift. Hope is life. No matter what you are going through, hope will give you the strength to hold on because your change will come.

Betty A. Funderburke, DTM
Absolutely Articulate Toastmasters #1272692
Aurorators #2136
bettyfunderburke@yahoo.com

Can You Hear Me Now?

If you are to make listening a profitable pursuit, you must first understand it. Perhaps you think you already do. Let's find out. The purpose of this article is to make you think about the importance of listening – what it is, and what it is not. Let's start by disposing of some false assumptions that pervade our subject.

With the exception of the deaf, most of us are born with two good ears and during our lifetime, we listen from 45% to 63% of the time. This percentage has been confirmed by research, and there's no denying its accuracy. The fact is, we spend nearly half our time listening. Add to this the fact that many of us are bad listeners, and the potential for improvement is limitless.

Although listening has been placed on the back burner in almost every book ever written on the art of communication, lately there is fresh hope that it will take its rightful place among the communicative skills, which is, as borne out by research . . . number one.

Can you hear me now?

Virginia Glist
Toast-a-Matics Toastmasters Club #1120162
vjglist@in2l.com

47

Relics ...

Running barefoot at night through rich soil of recent
plowed fields,
Trying to capture the secrets of lightning bugs in flight.

Witnessing a bright, sunny sky turn into ghostly, dark
clouds,
While thunder roared like a nearby cannon war,
And lightning danced perpetually near and far,
Crackling throughout the sky like a gigantic electric whip.

Watching a young bird struggling to fly for the first time,
Enjoying the beauty of its success as it soars
And disappears in a colossal foliage kingdom.

Sitting alone on a river bank,
Listening to wind songs from restless branches high in the
tree tops,
Or other soft multifarious tunes of nature.

Reaching endlessly into the darkest of nights,
Fearing that something may reach back,
Or feeling the presence of something unknown,
But with a sudden frightful turn, found myself completely
alone.

Lift As You Climb

➤ ❖

Inhaling the essence of the earth after a summer rain,
Smelled variegated spring flowers,
Or with a sudden shift of wind,
Inhaled the aroma of supper waiting at a distance.

Quivering from cold morning dew,
While plunging through a grassy meadow,
And the nip in the morning air reminds me that,
Once again, summer is almost over and autumn is only
days away.

Roaming through the remote wilderness of the countryside,
In search of sweet, drupaceous fruits of nature,
Spending an entire day, accomplishing little,
Losing only time.

Awakening in the early morning hours,
Wondering what happened to the world I once knew,
Eternal days and relics of yesterday.

Elizabeth Hall

Flying With Kamber . . .

Not so long ago, there lived a beautiful bouncing baby boy golden retriever named Kamber. He was my third Seeing Eye dog and while I loved the two before him, Kamber's recent death has been the hardest to grieve. Kamber gave me his unconditional love 24/7 for more than thirteen years. Unlike most people who leave their pets at home while they go to work every day, Kamber went everywhere with me. Now, three months after his death, people still ask me, "How's your pup," and I still get choked up when I tell them the story...

Kamber's little legs became weaker the last two months of his life. Our half-mile walks in the park became shorter, cutting them to a small stroll down a little hill to smell the grass and trees, then back home on the sidewalk for a couple of hundred steps. He loved his porch and spent every moment he could lying in the sun when the temperature was above 40 degrees. Most of the time he would go in and out, in and out, in and out, and in and out my front door driving me crazy; however, in hind sight, I'd do it all again, if allowing him to do that could bring him back.

On Thursday, February 24, 2011, the day after his 15 and a half birthday, Kamber stood up and fell down. After doing this several times, he ended up at the back door with his little nose lying in the crack between the frame and the screen. Even with his blue canvas harness with pull-up straps, I couldn't lift him. "You're okay, Kamber. You can lie there. I'll come back and check on you." I gave him a pat with lots of tears left him. Three hours later after I had made the fatal appointment for him at the vet's office, Kamber was walking around like nothing was wrong. He started going in and out (driving me nuts) and with gratitude, I canceled the appointment.

Friday came and went without incident; however, on Saturday, Kamber started getting up and falling down all over again. I hated to see his little leg curled up while he winced in pain. I crawled over to him and reached out my hand to comfort him; he moved away. "It's okay, I won't hurt you baby!" I called my friend, Rachel. "What shall we do? I don't want to give him to God, and I can't let him be in pain either!"

Rachel said, "I think it's time. How about you call the vet and see if they have time today?" I called and the next window of opportunity was Monday, February 28 at 7:00 AM. With heavy heart, I made the appointment. That afternoon was normal with Kamber going in and out in and out, and in and out my front door and lying in his beloved sun. I stayed inside watching him from my green glider.

The following morning, Kamber jumped to his feet as usual with no assistance from me. I gave him breakfast and afterwards brushed his ears, back, legs and tail. Every once in a while I would lean down and hug him sobbing into his fur, "This isn't for you, it's for me." He would breathe in and give me a contented long sigh.

At noon I went to a local restaurant for a rescheduled birthday party for Kamber and I. After the twenty people finished eating, I tapped my glass, "I want to thank you for coming. Kamber would have been here, but he didn't want to come. You all are like my family and I appreciate you in my life, loving and supporting me." I took in a deep breath with tears welling up in my eyes. "As you go around and introduce yourselves and how you know me, I want you to share a Kamber memory." I gulped. "Tomorrow, Kamber is going to go to God; it's time! His little legs are getting worse, and I don't want him to suffer any more. Please give your name, relationship to me and your memories."

Afterwards, Danette, Linda and Becky volunteered to come with me and Rachel the next morning to say good-bye to Kamber. That night, I sat on the floor and told Kamber my appreciations, regrets and hopes. "I appreciate everything about you. Your happy personality; your soft ears; your long silky hair; your love of treats and crackers; your playful spirit; tearing up my pants legs and wrapping paper when you were a puppy; everything. There's so many things I appreciate it's hard to think of them all. All the companionship you gave me going everywhere with me: grocery stores, shopping, restaurants, concerts, plays, people's homes. You were the best retired Seeing Eye dog on the planet. I regret teaching you to stop for every driveway when you were a Seeing Eye dog. I regret doing what I have to do tomorrow. I hope you go to God in peace and that you play with all the other dog angels. I hope you are without pain. I hope there is a Heaven! I hope you are happy and loved. I hope you miss me as much as I'll miss you. I hope we see each other again."

The next morning, Monday February 28 at 4:30 am, I climbed out of bed, dressed and had breakfast. Linda came at 5:45 and read a wonderful poem regarding dog heaven. As she told the story, I stroked Kamber's soft ears. There are angels in dog Heaven and they give treats to all the dogs. Kids play ball with all the dogs … They all sit when they are asked, for all dogs are good in dog Heaven. And they sleep on soft fluffy clouds going round and round until they find the perfect place to lie.

Just two days before, another friend told me a story of a woman who had a near death experience. She saw her dog and he showed her his "dog house." It was the way he always wanted it while on earth, a soft couch looking out a window. All of a sudden, the dog said, "I love you and want to stay with you, but I've got to dig."

"What?" The woman was perplexed.

"I got to go dig," and with that, he was off, then she came back into her body. Soon after, she found out that there had been an earthquake and knew that her dog was being asked to help people or dogs on earth save lives.

Alas, it was time to go. With ease, Kamber walked up his portable ramp and into Rachel's van. Linda, Rebecca, and Danette met us at the vet's office. There, the staff was wonderful touching my arm, speaking words of comfort and apology. We walked into our familiar examination room where a blanket had been placed on the floor. Dr. W. came in and described the procedure in a compassionate yet professional demeanor. He gave Kamber a sedative and left us alone. Every few minutes he'd come back, "is he getting sleepy? No? I'll be back." Meanwhile, Linda offered lovely poetry and a song of love and transition while Becky gave sweet touches, and Danette prayed as Rachel reached out with loving acts of kindness. All took on many roles; however, the experience though dreadfully difficult, was simply beautiful!

Kamber took ten to fifteen minutes to react to the sedative. "Atta boy Kamber - you stay awake. Do whatever you want." All the while, he went to everyone in our group nestling them and getting treats. He'd go over and drink water out of a bowl, "Atta boy Kamber, you eat and drink as much as you want." He only came to me at the end when he couldn't stay awake any longer. Sitting with his back to me, I reached out and felt his soft silky ears. "You're okay, Kamber; I love you." He finally lay on his tummy with his head up. "It's okay Kamber. You're okay." Stroking his ears, I sobbed.

Suddenly Dr. W. was sitting in front of me. "I'll soon give the drugs. He's getting sleepy. His eyes are closing." I felt his head; it was down. His soft ears were lying on his paws.

I stroked again. "I love you Kamber - Go to God."

"Are you ready?" I wasn't, and yet, I knew I had to let him go. "You have the furriest paws I've ever seen; you're a beautiful animal." I stroked those ears and sobbed.

"He's gone?" I felt his ribs.

"Yes," and with that, Dr. W. leaned over and gave me a hug while I caressed Kamber. For one hour while sobbing into his fur and stroking his beloved ears, I lingered with my baby boy.

Two days later I dreamed Kamber was in my house running back and forth skidding and sliding. "What do you have in your mouth?" I felt his mussel, and there was a baby bottle. "You are such a tease!! You always like to tease me!" I woke up laughing. I told myself, if there is a dog Heaven, just maybe my Kamber is up there running and teasing while waiting for me!

Kamber was a kind-hearted, gentle, loving boy. He loved popcorn while watching the Broncos; playing ball at my therapist's office; attending music performances; searching out for crumbs under the reception table afterwards; scrounging for scraps at music jam sessions; lying on the porch basking in the sun; digging in the snow; standing on his head and wiggling his butt in the air; rubbing his face on the carpet after a treat or while waiting to go to the park; wrapping himself around trees on his twenty-five foot flex-a-lead; going swimming; and so many other fun things.

Later, I had a second dream where we were walking perfectly in tandem together. Suddenly, instead of my left hand holding onto his harness handle, both my hands were holding tight to Kamber's collar. We were flying! With his front paws outstretched and his ears flapping in the breeze and my long red hair and legs flowing behind me, we flew like lightning. Faster and higher we went. As we reached the end of a long tunnel, I woke up. I believe Kamber was showing me that there is life after death and that he was indeed a happy boy. My greatest heart's desire is to fly, and Kamber showed me that indeed I will get my wings. These two dreams were God-sent gifts, and I am blessed and grateful for Kamber's life and for his death. And so to my precious beautiful bouncing Baby Boy I want to say, "Kamber, I'll love you forever." To my friends, "Thank you for your love and understanding of the special love I had for Kamber." And to everyone, if you are lucky and blessed enough to have a best buddy and companion like my Kamber, love him or her with all your heart and soul and recognize that best friends comes in all shapes and sizes.

Gail Hamilton
ToastAbility Toastmasters #863184
wingstofly@comcast.net

The Eeyore Effect. . .

"I'm moving to a state I never wanted to move to, work in an industry I never wanted to work in, and learn a trade I never wanted to have." Imagine my disappointment to hear my twenty five year-old son speak these defeatist words. After being unemployed for a year, he'd better be thankful for a chance to move to Casper, Wyoming, instead of sounding like. . .Eeyore.

It reminded me of times in my life when I faced job loss. I was a newly minted church music graduate. "I'll show up, love God, we'll hold hands and sing Kum ba Yah." With classes in graded choirs, handbells, recorders and choral conducting, I wasn't prepared for working with . . . the music committee. I even bumped heads with the pastors! After bouncing around in several jobs, each time thinking "surely the next one will be different," I was fired in 1988. I lost not only my job, but almost my ministry, my identity and my faith in people. More recently, I was laid off by a large corporation and remained unemployed for sixteen months. With more experience, more education and higher call volume than several others, I was the one laid off.

Many of you have probably faced similar unjust treatment, bad performance reviews, demotions or losses. Did you give yourself a pep talk? "This could be a great opportunity, and an exciting adventure, I'll meet new people, and learn new skills!" A little pep talk isn't going to make long-term changes if you're struggling with . . . the Eeyore Effect. What is it? More than being down in the dumps or having a blue day, the Eeyore Effect is a life view that establishes negativity and defeat as the daily mode of operation.

If only I'd known about it back in my days as a church musician. Instead, I fumbled along until I decided. "I don't want to feel bad anymore." A move to Denver and jobs in customer service led to some successes until the most recent down cycle. I moved my 85-year-old mother out here from Ohio and was laid off two months later. Thankfully, at this stage of my life I was able to find the hidden blessings. I got to have sixteen months of precious time Mom before she went into a nursing home. I got to take computer classes on a workforce grant, upgrading my skills. I got to participate in aqua-aerobics, getting in better shape.

When do you sound like Eeyore? Maybe what you need is to change the way you look at life. Oh sure, that's a snap. But what if it really is that easy? The advice I offer you today comes from years of life experience -- and therapy! The next time you hear defeatist and depressing words coming out of your mouth, you can choose to live under the Eeyore Effect or you can look for the hidden blessings! Change the way you think by saying, "I don't have to. I get to!"

Pamela Hertzog, AC-G, AL-B
Ranch Raconteurs Toastmaster #873616
pamela_hertzog@yahoo.com

Unpaid Debt. . .

I couldn't have asked for a better start,
What we didn't have in money, we made up for with heart,

Taught as a child that a good education,
Could prepare anyone for any destination,

But as much I love my family tree,
They weren't the first to pave the way for me,

Folks I've never met, did things I can't forget,
Those sacrifices could have equaled unpaid debt,

Like how our founding fathers laid such a solid foundation,
That some of the world's greatest advances happened
because of our nation,

Like how slaves risked their lives so I wouldn't have to risk
mine, and how Dr. King shared his dream after he saw a
sign,

Those are big shoes to fill and I always know,
I've got work to do before I go,

So you'll see me with a smile instead of a frown,
You'll see me helping Toastmasters all over town,

I can't let myself live selfishly or filled with regrets,
Because I've always believed in paying my debts.

Donna Hilton, CC
Aurorators Toastmasters #2136
Absolutely Articulate Toastmasters #1272692
donnahilton@ymail.com

8

Would you Share Three Minutes to Change the World?

"In three minutes, you can change the world."

I doubt 20 years ago that I would have believed that statement. Then I took my first cruise ship vacation. Being in a relaxed environment, I began my intense study of human nature. Here we will often show our true beauty and integrity to the world.

Well, I was hooked when I found that cruise lines needed "Kind Gentlemen" to share dances for the solo-traveling passengers. Now I was *really* hooked! Over the past 15 years for my vacations, I have spent over 220 days sharing dances. My duties were to be at all social events to teach or share a dance, give every lady in the room a chance to dance and rotate to the next smiling face. In exchange, I would get a free cruise. Cool!

Hawaii, Europe, Easter Island, South America and Antarctica were amazing, but it was always the people that brought the greatest memories to me. As each person appreciated a dance, I hadn't understood the possible impact until I met Margaret from Wales. She was traveling with her daughter and three granddaughters.

Margaret and I were dancing to the famous song by Glenn Miller, *In the Mood*. About halfway through, I could feel Margaret's whole body change. Although her face went pale, her feet kept moving briskly to the music. I feared a major medical problem, and started scanning the room for the ship's doctor. When the song ended, Margaret would not let go of my hand as I returned her to her seat. She insisted that I stay to hear her story. She recalled the exact moment 43 years earlier when she and her husband danced to that same song. She spoke of the town, the dance hall, the weather and even how they were dressed. Margaret delivered her personal, passionate story with great joy and a tear in her eye. She later told me how she enjoyed the trip with her girls, the sights, and the meals; however, it was the three minutes with me on the dance floor that made her trip. It changed her world.

I believe we all should be given three minutes to change the world.

Tom G. Hobbs, DTM
Gates to Excellence Toastmasters #3413
dancetom@comcast.net

Not Speaking Up. . .

I don't always speak up. It would be helpful if I would talk, but a conversation in my head holds me back. It's usually because I don't want to hurt anyone's feelings. My silence sometimes convinces others to call me "non-judgmental." That's not entirely true. I hold back around people who are older than me; I'm afraid of them. Complete strangers: I pretend to agree with whatever they say. Sometimes I see all sides of a thing and it's hard to let them know.

When you are an agreeable, accommodating person as I am, you're often at the receiving end of bizarre confessions, unreasonable requests and downright crazy and/or unpleasant situations. When you can't speak up, it steers you funny every time.

My sister, Chris, and I took a cruise for her birthday last year. We wanted to have fun and meet new people. Our first morning at sea, we went to breakfast in a fancy dining room. "You will be seated at a table with others, ok?" But they didn't say it like a question. Truly it felt more like *"No thank you, we'd rather not,"* but that would have been the wrong thing to say. There was something in the way they said it, or the way they looked at us, I don't know; so we agreed. Besides, we were there to have fun and meet new people.

It was not to be.

Instead, we sat across from Hans (a pensioned-off retiree) who was an experienced cruiser from the upper Midwest, having been on forty trips all over the world to exotic locations like Capetown and Dubrovnik. That part of the conversation proved to be just fine; however, my problem started when it came time to order our meal.

Hans advised us "newbies" that we could order as many breakfasts as we wanted, and practically commanded me to do so. He even informed me that if I wanted ten platters of sausages, they would unquestioningly bring them to me. For the record, I did not (nor do I now - nor will I ever) want to eat ten platters of sausages in one go. Horrified, we ate our lady-portions of healthy fruit and oatmeal, as Hans demonstrated for us the deadly sin of gluttony, with grease gleaming on his chin in the morning light.

I wanted to stand up and shout "PUT DOWN THAT FORK, YOU WRETCHED OLD MAN!" But I just couldn't. Hans was old, and I can never speak up around old people. Instead, Chris and I ate quickly and hurriedly took our leave.

We probably could have refused to be seated with other parties, but for the rest of the trip we enjoyed room service and chose to have breakfast in private on our balcony. We never did meet anybody.

That's what you get for not speaking up.

Joan Janis
Cherry Creek Toastmasters #2977
joan@bretztec.com

Manners . . .

What are manners? Manners are a way of doing something or the way in which a thing is done or happens; a way of acting; bearing or behavior; the socially correct way of acting; etiquette. We start to learn manners as early as the toddler years. Right? Maybe not everyone!

Some of us were taught to say please when asking for that cookie or toy. After receiving what was given, we always knew to say "thank you." As we grew up past the toddler years, we learned to say "excuse me" if we wanted to pass by someone. We also learned that "excuse me" meant a move in a particular situation. We learned to say "I'm sorry" if we offended someone or hurt someone's feelings. During our learning years, we began to accept apologies from others. Remember?

As we became teenagers and learned how to drive, we gained yet another lesson: courtesy. For example, when someone lets you over into a lane, what normally happens? You raise your hand, which represent a nonverbal thank you!

I've always been taught that it was rude to ask a woman or man their age. I didn't really understand until this weekend. Why? My stepson and I went to a baby shower, and I was talking to a lady next to me. My stepson decided to jump into our conversation without saying excuse me, and asked her age. He asked, "How old are you? Are you 99 years old?" Now, this comment took her by surprise. In the midst of her shock, he then, "You really look 78 years old." Now at this point he is thinks he's giving her a compliment. After coming out of her shock she asked him if he had ever met a 78-year-old. He added, "yes and since you are both the same height, you must be the same age." Of course, being a child, he was merely trying to be polite and pay her a compliment.

I think along the way some of us may have lost a few of the things we were taught early on. One example would be with customer service. How many times have you gone through a checkout line and the cashier has not acknowledged you at all?

Let me take this opportunity to give you a few things to remember about good manners:

1. Using the terms "thank you," "please" and "you're welcome" indicates good manners. People lacking in manners avoid these terms.
2. Greet others appropriately, even if you know someone well. If you are a man, you do not want to greet a woman by saying, "Hey baby, what's shaking?" Instead, try something like, "Hello," "good morning (or evening)" -- anything making you appear respectful.
3. Don't put others down, belittle them, or spread gossip. Never criticize someone in an attempt to demean or to elevate yourself.

4. Don't interrupt, cut off or override others, unless they are insulting or swearing, etc. Give others respect and try letting them finish; be a listener -- and practice being a *good* one!

5. Bonus: When someone says hello, say hello back.

Remember that poor manners are a reflection of you, your family and the company you represent. Don't forget that the purpose of good manners is to help.

Iffie Jennings
Aurorators Toastmasters #2136
iffieg@hotmail.com

My First Speeding Ticket. . .

Before talking about my first speeding ticket, I would like to give all of you a short introduction of who I am. I was born and raised in a sweet and a peaceful little town in the southern part of India. The name of our little town was Siruvani, with a population of about 750 people. This town has a wonderful view of mountains and rivers and wild life. I used to watch wild elephants strolling with their little ones together on the river banks. I also enjoyed various birds, especially peacocks, dancing in the rice fields.

Why did I leave my beautiful town? My passion for healthcare and interest to pursue an education in this country encouraged me to leave my little town of Siruvani and ultimately brought me to Denver, Colorado.

The first six months were pretty interesting as I had many, many second thoughts, debating hard within myself and wondering if I had made the right decision coming to this country. Even though there were so many thoughts going on in my mind, I decided to get my driver's license. My instructor told me that I was driving pretty well and was eligible for a driver's license. Now I am not taking the bus to my work; I am driving. Even though everybody warned me to be careful, I did not feel any difference, nor was I nervous driving on the highway. But heck yeah!! Other drivers on the road felt for me. I was curious why everyone was in a big hurry, and sensed that every driver wanted to say something to me and, although many of them did, I apparently did not understand what was being communicated. All that finger language, shouting and swearing language! Because I did not understand these sometimes strange, nonverbal and verbal languages, nothing really mattered for me. Days went by like this. On one occasion when I was following a friend to a party, she called me and asked if I was experiencing car problems. When I asked why, she responded that I was driving so slowly. Later at the party, Kumu's driving was the topic of the night. Of course, I was teased by many at the party when they found out that I had been driving so slowly on the highway.

After that, I realized my mistake and I started driving faster. This time, the direction of my speedometer changed, inching up towards 90- 95 miles per hour. Not only that, I was driving in the left-most HOV lane. I also enjoyed overtaking other cars which was fun, or so I thought. For a while, I was enjoying this style of driving until I was surrounded by a few police cars. At that time, I did not know about undercover (unmarked) police cars. I always identified police cars painted with white and blue colors. When the undercover police were following, I did not stop my car for a few miles. Apparently, one policeman called others for assistance. I ended up in a situation where the white car was literally chasing me in the HOV lane. As soon as I saw the white car, I slammed my brakes stopping my car with a loud, screeching noise.

Next I heard a loud sound that said, "Move to the right - move to the right." I was so curious to know why the police voice was so loud and why he could not hear me. Later I figured out that he had a special microphone that he was using. Now the drama starts. I still remember the blue eyes of the policeman who was so angry. The cop approached me, and asked me if I realized what I did. I was choked up, so I just shook my head. The next question he asked was if I knew English. I slowly responded, "yes." He told me that he needed to take my license away since I had broken a number of driving laws. He also told me that they had been chasing me for a while. I explained that I did not notice anything unusual and was unaware that I was been chased. Needless to say, the officer took my license, insurance and other documents. I said in a pitiful voice tone, "sorry officer - I made a mistake." He responded in a very loud voice, "Come again?" This time with tears dripping from my eyes, I said, "Sorry, sir." Meanwhile I was showing him all kinds of identification including my work ID, student id and other personal identification. While noticing that I was being stared at as if I was crazy, I explained that this would be my first speeding ticket.

The police officer walked back to his car and when he came back, he told me that the ticket would be $800 dollars plus 12 points. I was adamant, and refused to sign the paperwork. He retreated again and this time, he came back with a fine of $800 and dropped the points to zero. I asked him if he would be willing to get me a job to enable me to pay the $800. Once again, he went back to his car and returned with a reduced fine of $50. Amazed that police in America work in this manner, I said, "That sounds better." He smiled at me and said, "You must promise me, lady that you will never drive this fast again!" I assured him that I would do as he asked, and to this day, I have not taken the HOV lane even if I have a passenger in my car.

The moral of the story is this: You can be ignorant once in your life, but it is very important that you gain knowledge and use it wisely. Also, it is important to be truthful to others as well as to yourself. Although we all make mistakes, we should try not to repeat them; however if mistakes occur, speak up and fight for yourself.

I truly was unaware of the undercover police in unmarked cars. What a lesson that I learned on that day!

Kumu Keindaswami
Absolutely Articulate Toastmasters #1272692
gkkumu@gmail.com

Never Give Up . . .

As a child, I longed for brothers and sisters. My family consisted of my elderly, adoptive parents and me. My adopted father died when I was three, and then there was just Mama and me for 11 more years. I was a lonely, solitary child. I knew I had to have a family of origin somewhere, and it became a burning desire within me to locate them.

After I married and had two children, I became curious about family traits, and I wondered about family resemblances. As I grew older, I wondered what medical conditions and genetic time-bombs lurked in the unknown family tree. I began a search for my birth family with high hopes. I knew some searches were not successful, and I knew some birth parents did not want to be found. I knew that, but I had hope and optimism in abundance. I had no idea that my search would take over 46 years of dead ends and frustration. I considered giving up more times than I can remember.

My daughter was curious, and always motivated me to start again after a painful let-down. She had children by then, and there were even more curious family traits showing up in our small, but growing family. My daughter was willing to take on the search, and begged me to let her do so. I refused to let her complete what I had started. I could not give up.

In August of 2009, I advertised for a "search angel" to help me locate my mysteriously non-existent family. A woman in California answered my plea, and used her computer and genealogical skills on my behalf. For four days and nights, she and I sat at our computers and churned thru data previously unavailable to me. We were successful! We found my family! I am so glad that I had not given up.

I now have thirteen-plus sisters and brothers. I was not the only one given up for adoption, and no one knows how many of us there actually are. We are still searching for others. I have met and formed relationships with five siblings, and correspond with four more. One is strange and unfriendly, but the others are delightful, and my life is greatly enriched by their addition to my life.

Forty-six years of a painful and frustrating search is over. Now I am free to get to know the people I always knew existed. I learned to my surprise and joy that during the time I searched for them, they also searched for me. My problem had been that I had been given false paperwork and false names. My birth parents did not want to be found, but my siblings want me in their lives.

I have learned two truths to share with you when you are stuck:

1. Never give up. The rewards are greater than the obstacles.
2. Ask for help.

Oh, and did I mention? Never give up!

Pattie Koop
Pioneer Toastmasters #2932
askpattie@gmail.com

Little Ray of Sunshine . . .

Penmanship class, the Ark of the Covenant and the dinosaur: what do they all have in common? They are recorded in history but basically unknown in the present day ... handwritten thank you notes follow close behind.

Writing notes of appreciation and encouragement is almost a lost art. It is certainly far less frequent than it was a generation ago. I am showing my age. We all dash a fast email or text now rather than sending a hand written note. Not so long ago, it was considered very poor manners not to write a note of appreciation for a kind gesture, a gift or even a special dinner invitation. Now most of these are either ignored totally or given a quick email response. Amy who? Emily who? What's their Twitter or Facebook ID? Do you even recognize the names Amy Vanderbilt or Emily Post? Etiquette books? Yes, people actually read and studied their books.

Little notes of appreciation are so important that most of us have saved them in a scrapbook, a drawer or even a box. The point is that we saved them. I know I did. Notes are even more valuable when they were unexpected.

Who would love a note of appreciation from you? Just a little two line note which would not take you but a few minutes to write, address the envelope and mail. It is easy to do. The problem is that, as the noted business philosopher, Jim Rohn, says, "It is easy to do, but it is also easy not to do."

Walt Whitman, American poet, essayist, humanist, and journalist was struggling to receive recognition for his work when he received a note. The simple note said, "I am not blind to the wit and wisdom of the *Leaves of Grass*. I greet you at the beginning of a great career," signed Ralph Waldo Emerson. Walt kept that note. Not only was it a note of encouragement but it was from Emerson, the man who inspired Walt to write Leaves of Grass. Whitman spent his entire life writing and rewriting *Leaves of Grass*. It was first published in 1855, when Whitman was 36. Thirty six was the beginning of his great career.

Little notes of encouragement and inspiration to keep moving forward are sometimes the fine line that provides one more burst of energy for the recipient. How would you feel if you knew your little two line note was the one extra spark that propelled someone to achieve their dreams instead of giving up? Many give up moments before they crest the summit of an obstacle and revel in the glory of all of their hard work. One person believing in them and taking the time to let them know can be the difference between success and quitting.

Who needs a little two-line note of encouragement or appreciation from you? Write down the names of three people who deserve a note from you, commit to writing those three little notes and then do it.

You may never know how much it meant to them. That little ray of sunshine you poured into their life may inspire them to do the same for three others. Who knows how much joy we could spread in this world by taking the time to write three little notes? Look what it did for Whitman.

Elaine Love, DTM
Meridian Mid Day Toastmasters #7326
Spirited Speakers Toastmasters #1440289
Speak Up Toastmasters #6015
resultsforlife@gmail.com

The Greatest of These is Love. . .

I moved to Colorado from Louisiana about a year and a half ago. Although it was extremely hard leaving everything I had ever owned behind, I knew, if I was to ever become who I was supposed to be, that I had to do this. I am not sure if it was the beautiful mountains, the special time here or exactly what it was, but I do know that I have developed a new love for people. This renewed sense of appreciation and love for my family are spiritual treasures that I never knew previously existed. Why? Because I cared more about being important and perceived as the status quo, I was busy chasing "things."

I will never forget hearing my Grandmother on her death bed speaking to me. While I never heard her talk about how much money she had or what cars they owned or where they lived, I only heard about sweet memories that God had blessed her with. Grandmother reflected on thoughts from long ago about those who had gone on before her and memories of those she was leaving. Love is what her special memories were all about. Blessed with the special gift of discernment, my Grandmother knew what loving people right where they were was all about. Instead of waiting until they became what she wanted them to be, she saw way past where they were and what they could become. She cautioned me that since the people I love will not always be near me, I must seize the opportunity now and cherish them before it is too late.

The marvelous thing about love is that it is contagious and comes with a ripple effect. Hurting people always upsets them, and if there is one thing I know for sure, it is that every one of us is hurting in one way or another. When people are in distress, it is sometimes because they are scared. Over the past couple of years, I have realized that most people just want to feel like they matter and that somebody really cares about them. Since then, I now ask people how they are; then I remain quiet long enough to hear them share how they really feel. Since we don't know what "hurt" looks like, how do we know who is or isn't hurting? We don't - but if we would only slow down long enough to seize the opportunity to become real with ourselves and others, we might begin to experience love at its deepest level. In spite of what you may hear or see, none of us were made to be islands. Unfortunately, some of us walk past people on a daily basis that are dying on the inside because they have not experienced love.

Do you want to be the change that our world needs? Because each of us is holding the passport to that change, I suggest that we all start using it now! Friends, all of us have choices. Think about it: each night before we go to bed, we hear of millions of men, women and children across the globe that are starving, but have you ever thought about all of the families right here, probably within your arms' reach, who are also starving for a "kind word" or just a "simple smile"? Will you be the bold and caring one that gives it to them? My personal goal is to continue being one of those who extend love and compassion to those who need to hear and feel that others care about them. In years past, I sometimes coped with life by feeling sorry for myself. However, today I say "No more!" I've decided that it's time to stand up, speak out and share what I have with others. When we do this, I believe that we will end up with much more than we started out with.

Today, let's begin to embrace our lives and embrace each other with love, absent of expectations and pre-conceived ideas. There is a gentleman that I know who goes by the name of "Overtime." After he greets me, he always reminds me of who I am. Right now, I can hear him saying, "Good morning, champion." Wow! As a result of seeing ourselves differently, it's no telling what could be accomplished if we would only take on a positive outlook on life. Friends, in just one year and a half, my life has taken a dramatic turn for the better that will have a lasting and meaningful impact on everyone that I encounter. To everyone I meet, I say "if we meet and you forget me, you have lost nothing. But if you meet Jesus Christ and forget Him, then you have lost everything." No matter how unreasonable, illogical and self-centered people are, I encourage you today to love them without reservation.

In some small way, I hope and pray that this story I have shared has encouraged, inspired and motivated you to be the best version of yourself that you can be. I agree with these words by poet Maya Angelou who once said, "I have learned that people will forget what you said, people will forget what you did, but people will never forget how you made them feel."

Stephanie Lynn, CC
Absolutely Articulate Toastmasters #1272692
stephanielynnspeaking@yahoo.com

Personal Transformation...

Who Am I? Sounds like a very simple question to answer ... doesn't it? This is the question that I had been ignoring for most of my life. At this very moment as I am writing this summary of about who I am, I realize that I have not taken the time to get to know myself as well as I should. Although there was never enough time to take on this great feat to understand who I am, life gave me an opportunity through a life-changing event that served as the catalyst to help me unravel this complicated web.

As a child, I was privileged to grow up in a loving and caring family; however, like many families, there were certain family behavior dynamics that were dysfunctional. Some of these dysfunctional, negative family behaviors impacted how I felt about myself resulting in self doubt and internal fear. Although my family's love outweighed the negativity, it was apparent that my family's awareness of the impact of these dysfunctional behaviors was not clearly understood. Because I grew up feeling that I wasn't good enough and needed to prove myself, I found comfort when I excelled in school, thus showing off my intellectual gifts. As an excellent student in mathematics, I took great interest in pursuing a career as an engineer. How fortunate I was when both my parents (and math instructor) encouraged me to pursue my dreams. As a result of my pursuit for excellence, I was the first family member to graduate from college (New Mexico State University), where I received my Bachelors of Science Degree in electrical engineering. After college, I was once again fortunate to be hired by a major corporation where I worked as a systems engineer. Indeed I had achieved my childhood dream!

Although I found exercising my IQ to be very rewarding in my role as a student and engineer, I still experienced a visible gap in my soul because I was incapable of understanding my heartfelt feelings that were connected with who I am.

On January 28, 2005, I experienced a life changing event that gave me the opportunity to put aside engineering and begin to untangle the web of who I am. One evening while at home working on my computer, I suddenly felt a sharp pain on the right side of my ribs. Believing that I could be having a heart attack, my ex-wife and children found me in pain and quickly rushed me to the nearest hospital. While in the emergency room, everything seemed to be taking place in slow motion; it was surreal. I felt like this was the day that I was going to die!

As I assessed my life over the years, all I could think about was I didn't have time to say goodbye to everyone I loved - especially my children, parents and ex-wife. I realized that I had taken life, my health and my relationships with those I love for granted. On January 28, 2005, I asked God for a second chance.

While testing revealed that I had not a heart attack, my cholesterol and sugar levels were at a dangerously high level that was supported by a plethora of stress and anxiety. I realized that I had turned into a dying "couch potato" who was lethargic, overweight and without any energy. My eating habits included fast food along with very little vegetables or water. Additionally, my diet was not balanced and the negative self talk was at an all time high.

The choice was clear. I would decide to change or face continuance down the path leading to the field of daisies where I was destined to become the fertilizing agent! Because I made the decision to live, I also chose to light *the internal flame* needed to fulfill my heartfelt desire to become healthy and live a better life.

As a result of this decision, I focused on learning the value of hydration, eliminating contaminants, exercise and food selection. Most of all, I learned how important it was to think good thoughts while surrounding myself with good, positive people. I also discovered the importance of learning the body's language to feel and express my positive and creative feelings in everything I do. Finally, I discovered that our internal spirit requires a regular, ample dose of love and gratitude in order to achieve ultimate health and happiness.

I would like to take this opportunity to thank my beloved children (Alicen and Vidal), and their mother for helping me during my life-changing experience. I would also like to thank members of my Toastmasters family for giving me the opportunity to be a part of this exciting literary book project. As a result of my personal transformation, I have finally been able to unravel the web of discovering who I am through meditation and self awareness while growing closer to God. Every day is now an adventure that I look forward to with hope and optimism. To our book reading audience, I challenge each of you to make better decisions needed to discover new and improved health and vitality. Cheers!

Jose "George" Maestas
Simply Speaking Toastmasters #677476
Absolutely Articulate Toastmasters #1272692
george@greenh2owell.com

Bullying. . .

I am a 14-year-old high school student in Colorado. I am writing to make you aware of a serious problem that I recently faced regarding mean-spirited students who have made life rough for me and other students. As I see it, bullying has gone way too far because it stands to hurt too many kids! As a result, many of us have been left experiencing horrible emotions like hatred, sadness, anger and lots of hurt.

Hurt also happens when kids make fun of other kids on the internet. Now young people in our world are suffering even more from what is going on with cyber bullying, as well. Because kids have been experiencing all kinds of bullying for years, we are sick and tired of it. I personally knew a kid who was known to be a bully; later he started cyber bullying. Although it may appear to be fun to the bully, I encourage you to never get involved in this type of activity because it makes those being targeted feel very bad about themselves. Wouldn't it be nice if we had a website that helped to prevent kids from participating in cyber bullying? If we could somehow show what other kids actually feel like when they are bullied, the bully might stop it and start to become a nicer person.

Any kind of bullying is *not* okay because it hurts the kids more than the person doing the bullying! When I hear of kids being teased by bullies, it hurts from the inside out because I was intimidated by bullies from the first grade all the way to the ninth grade. I know first-hand how horrible it feels. Finally, in the 8th grade, both my brother and I were sexually harassed. Because we reported this incident to my teacher, principal and superintendent, it stopped right away; as a matter of fact, the kids who were involved in this incident were all suspended. Since I have been a victim of bullying, I know how awful it makes the other person feel and would never do such a thing! It hurts even more when you are a student at school because you are teased and harassed in front of all of your friends.

Bullying comes in all shapes and sizes: there is sexual harassment, sexual assault, verbal abuse, physical abuse, indirect abuse, intimidation; I could go on and on and on! I was just thinking: in order to stop cyber bullying, all of us should try to think of some creative ways that can stop this horrible problem. Perhaps we should consider making a Facebook page and invite people to join the group. I sometimes wonder if people doing the bullying was ever bullied themselves, and as a result, he or she thinks that it is okay to harass other people. If kids were kind and respectful to each other, I believe that this would never happen. Another suggestion is to start a support group that discourages people from bullying others. This will hopefully discourage others from thinking about going in this negative direction of hurting others. If people join and start to like this positive support group, maybe it will affect the bullies and it will be put to a stop. In other words, a group like this would make it clear to the bullies that they aren't powerful enough to hurt others. Because people who participate in bullying don't care about others or themselves, we need more students that speak out against this horrible problem!

Because it appears as if very few people are speaking out on the issue of bullying, I am hurt when I see so many young people suffering. Although bullying still happens at my school, I am happy to report that when I made those in authority aware of the problem, they immediately handled it. On the other hand, I have personally witnessed students who were hurt and scared by bullies. As I see it, these students who serve as bullies today will likely grow up and do the same thing as adults. Although I live in Colorado, my gut tells me that this disgusting problem is happening all over the world. One of my concerns is that kids who tell adult authorities about the bullies will be hurt again by the same bad guys, just to get even. Of course, many of these kids will never be the same after they get beat up by a bully because it lowers their self-esteem and is very embarrassing.

Thank you for letting me vent about this very real problem taking place at my high school and all across our country. Let's face it, because many choose to turn their head, the problem is not going away but getting bigger. Hopefully some of my ideas will be used to try to fix this serious problem. After all, if we don't speak out, the problem will remain and keep all of us worried, including those who are being bullied, those who are witnesses or assistants to bullying, and those who bully.

Katey McEniry
Friend of Absolutely Articulate Toastmasters #1272692

My Beautiful Obstacle. . .

I cannot believe that you are pregnant! What are you going to do with your life? I can still hear my mother asking me those questions with disappointment and frustration in her voice. At the time being only 19 years old, I didn't know what I was going to do. All I knew was that I was having a baby. I knew I wanted to be somebody, but what exactly did that mean?

April 16, 1991 changed my life forever. My baby girl was born and now I was a mother. I knew at that time that I wanted to be someone she could be proud of; someone that she could look up to. The cards were already stacked against me being a young, black, single mother, with only a high school education. I remember the negative comments from older women, telling me that my life was over and that I would never amount to anything because I had had a child so young. They said, "How are you going to attend college with a child? All you're going to do is have another baby and be on social services the rest of your life!" Really? Apparently, that is all they saw in me. However, I saw so much more...

I did become a welfare recipient, but I used what they gave me to my advantage. I decided to attend college when my daughter was three years old, without child care assistance. I attended the Community College of Denver and then a year and a half later, I was accepted into the University of Colorado at Boulder. What an accomplishment for a single mother! My daughter accompanied me to Boulder and attended classes with me my first year. Once she turned 5, she entered kindergarten and no longer attended morning classes with me. In May of 1999, "we" graduated from CU Boulder with a degree in Communication. Before I graduated, I prayed that God would bless me with a job before graduation, so I would know exactly where I would be going after school, and He did. I became a UNIX engineer for Sun Microsystems. I know it is completely different than what I went to college for, but when God gives it to you, He will see you through it. Everyone was extremely proud of me - even the naysayers. Little did they know that they were my motivation; however, my biggest motivator was my "beautiful obstacle" named TaVon Davis. She is and still remains one of the reasons I work so hard in all that I do. I now have two more additions that I work very hard for and their names are Brendon Walker II and Kennedy Walker. I have a great support system which includes my three children and my supportive husband. Having such a great support system has allowed me to return to higher education and receive my graduate degree. After graduating with a Masters in Human Resources in June, 2010, I elected to go back to school to pursue a second graduate degree in Management and Leadership.

Obstacles are things that impede progress or achievement. I have never looked at my children as obstacles, but society has. Use your "obstacles to your advantage. In the famous words of Frederick Douglass, "without struggle, there is not progress." I have struggled and I have progressed in my life and my career. Thanks to my beautiful obstacles for motivating me to be a better person and someone you could look up to and be proud of.

Who or what is your obstacle? Allow your situation to motivate you to overcome adversity and be thankful for your beautiful obstacles.

Troi Mullins
Absolutely Articulate Toastmasters #1272692
troi.mullins@gmail.com

Corazon du Janus Pan. . .

And when your heart is broken,
Let the pieces fall into the sea of tears.
They will reform
Into something scarred,
And so bigger,
The poisons of pain washed away.
After weeks, months or years,
It will tire of tears.
And being bored, numb, still scared,
It will rise.
Slowly perhaps,
But rise again it will.
And stronger,
Still scarred,
But near pain free.
Wiser, and swollen with saline tears turned to blood red
blood,
Hungry for a new love.
Heart looks for a new love.
But looking anew,
Looking for a lover,
It sees the loveless,
The hopeless.
And with a wiser, kinder, love,

Ever moving towards The *Light*.
Looking through others' tears,
Into and through their eyes,
It sees itself.
And remembering the magic of a stranger's hug,
Clasped hand,
Soft touch on the sleeve,
Or mere encouraging smile,
Stops to connect,
Give comfort, then moves away.
Only to discover that it is flying,
Lighter than before.
Looking back,
Heart sees the other,
Floating a little higher.
Then notices that it is looking past the flutter
Of its own slowly forming wings.
Thus beginning to acknowledge
The Divinity Within
Laughing, heart really begins to soar.

Edwin Pens
Gates to Excellence Toastmasters #3413
Ed.Pens@yahoo.com

You Are Not Alone. . .

At age thirteen, I had been a victim of bullying for two long years. Different kids at my school of various races, genders, social backgrounds, etc. were the perpetrators. I noticed something that these aggressive busybodies all had in common - they all came from dysfunctional homes. In addition to lots of physical and verbal abuse, I also noticed that my self-esteem was seriously affected. On one occasion, I remember being cornered in the locker room while these bad-spirited youngsters made fun of my clothes. I used to wear the neatest clothing, including the puffy skirts, and cute hair styles. One of hardest challenges for me was changing my complete appearance to avoid being harassed.

My recommendation to kids who are being victimized by bullies is to be honest with yourself and talk to your parents or a guardian. You can also get help by talking to your friends, teachers, counselors or principal. In my particular case, some of the teachers and principal were on the opposite side, but I didn't stop there. My counselor ended up being my best advocate.

The bottom line is that you *must* have someone to intercede for you! If you are a victim of bullying, I encourage you to call the Safe2Tell Hotline (1-877-542-7233), or go to their website (safe2tell.org). If you are not comfortable talking to an adult, please know that you can talk to a teen. My advice to victims of bullies is to talk about it, and know that you are not alone!

Cassie Perkins
Daughter of Absolutely Articulate Toastmasters Member #1272692
cassiopeia3@q.com

It's Okay to Cry. . .

Being a mom of two girls, I never thought my child-rearing knowledge would be used this way. Every fiber of my mental psyche, physical restraining ability and religion has been challenged and called upon when I learned that my oldest daughter was victimized. No, not sexual abuse – but mental and physical torture that she endured for two long years of her young life.

Every morning, I was awakened by my own sobbing and that of my daughter's to start my day, as she fearfully yet willingly prepared to go to school. The stories were unreal. While praying and seeking a solution to my daughter's very real problem, I finally told myself that it was okay to cry.

As strange as this sounds, my first encounter with the school system was met with denial, resistance and hopelessness. After many, many visits to my daughter's school, I followed through with all of the recommended courses of action. As a means to reach out and help my beloved, first-born daughter, I inundated myself in all the new information offered to me by the professionals in order to become more knowledgeable about what was going on in my daughter's life - only to discover that it was falling on deaf ears by the existing support system.

After learning that the children who taunted and tortured my daughter were from dysfunctional homes (connected with alcohol, drug and physical abuse), it became clear that they were also victims who chose to work out their problems by victimizing others. It was also plain to see that these misguided children with mental health problems (who the system refers to as "bullies") received their fuel, guidance, support, lack of love and attention from that same dysfunctional source – the home.

On many occasions, my family and I wanted to throw up our hands and give up, but while teaching her courage and wisdom, I could not let my young daughter face this nightmare alone. Because we were finally blessed to find other sources of support, we ultimately found permanent relief and resolution by removing my daughter from the school system. Although there were no consequences for the children who initiated the bullying, our family was relieved when we no longer had to face the daily battle of fighting the system even though we were clearly the victims.

To parents who may face similar challenges in the school system with their child(ren) who are victims of bullying, I encourage them to use every support resource that is available. First of all, talk to your child and be prepared to listen to him/her. Secondly, do not ignore their cries for help. If your child is shy or withdrawn, ask probing questions then seek help from teachers, counselors and school administrators. If you or your child are not taken seriously, be prepared to take the next step and continue probing further until you satisfactorily find resolution. This could include consulting the school board or publicly taking this matter to the press.

Today in the media, we hear, read and see on a daily basis stories similar to what happened to my daughter all over the country. This cold and senseless abuse based on a child's race, gender, economic position, social status, etc. must stop! I ask myself, "How could teens have so much hate in their hearts?" I feel that the system failed me as a parent and as a responsible tax-paying citizen. I not only took my daughter out of the school system, but I placed her in a home school program.

To the school principal and teachers, I demand that you stand up and speak out on behalf of our children - our future leaders. I am proud to say that my daughter is now part of a movement offering young people an opportunity to speak out about bullying and other important issues that they may face during this delicate time in their lives. Now, my oldest daughter responsibly and boldly speaks out to the media, other children, parents and educators as a means to educate them about the long-term danger of bullying – demeaning, abusive, aggressive behavior that involves unwanted, negative, repeated actions toward another person who cannot defend him/herself.

Right now, my daughter represents one of the voices for many of the boys and girls who have not or will not speak up for themselves. Single-handedly, she is making a difference while taking back her independence and self-confidence. Until the road to bullying has been permanently demolished, she has agreed to be one of the young voices. Meanwhile as her mother (and friend), I am very proud of her courage while teaching me and others that although it's okay to cry, it feels much better to stand up and speak out.

Joni Perkins
Absolutely Articulate Toastmasters #1272692
Joniperkins7436@msn.com

While Riding Through The Storm...

What have I done with my life? What did I want out of life? These are questions that I asked myself.

I could not believe how the time had passed me by so quickly. The feeling of disappointment and self-destruction came over me like the raging winds and dark clouds of a devastating storm. I realized that if I did not do something fast this deadly storm was going to consume me.

I was a single parent still living at home with my parents, running the streets all hours of the night as if I were homeless and doing drugs, which left lots of financial debt. You name it - I had it. Yeah, I had a real problem.

On one particular night in the midst of my personal storm, I was on my knees crying out for help. On this night, I prayed and asked God for forgiveness and deliverance from this monstrous demon that had a hold on me. At that very moment, I instantly felt the sun beaming over my face that left me with an overpowering sense of joy, hope, peace and happiness.

I was delivered! I AM delivered! Needless to say, I have never been the same since the day that I felt the Son.

Although I am no ways close to being where I want to be, I am thankful to God that I am not where I used to be. I personally believe that If He can do it for me, surely He can do it for you too.

In the midst of darkness, remember that there is always light. All you have to do is *believe*! While riding through your storms in life, always look for the Son; He is always there for you.

Praise be to God!

Denette Polk
Aurorators Toastmasters #2136
Nette1315@yahoo.com

Lift As You Climb. . .

Mama always said the greatest love is God, others and ourselves. How many of you believe that our life is determined by the way in which we react to the things that happen around us? The words for the day are *never stop trying,* and should you encounter someone who says something negative or tells you that you can't do something, let the attack roll off your back like water on glass and prove them wrong by trying even harder to do your best.

Mama encouraged us to be mindful of our reputation by being honest, sincere and dependable; she also reminded us to leave things better than we found them. No matter what job we're working on, she told me and her other eight children that we must make every effort to "lift as we climb." If you haven't already, discover your wings and prepare to fly high realizing that to get something you never had, you have to do something you never did. Remember that we can't fly with eagles if we hang with turkeys, so watch who you associate with and what comes out of your mouth.

Toastmasters, life is too short to wake up with regrets, so reach out and help those around you. Because our word is our bond, when you accept a task, go the distance and finish it. While representing the world's undisputed expert in communication and leadership skills development, I challenge you to make your profound mark on the world and make your Toastmasters International colleagues proud of you. And remember . . . be careful what you say and how you say it because once gone, time, words and opportunity never come back. Because it is impossible to take back our words (the most powerful drug used by mankind) once we've said them, I encourage you to first think about it, then stand up and speak out as polished, articulate, caring public speakers. After all, the world needs more smart and compassionate leaders. Quoted from the Good Book, "The wise in the heart shall be called prudent; and the sweetness of the lips increaseth learning." (Proverbs 16:21)

Stand up, toastmasters and friends and keep on standing while making a firm commitment to reach out and help others as you make your individual steps toward self improvement. Since it's hard to lose when you're on your feet, don't stop moving! Finally, I leave you with these golden, powerful words by Albert Einstein: "The world is too dangerous to live in not because of the people who do wrong, but because of the people who sit back and let it happen."

Elinora L. Reynolds, DTM
Absolutely Articulate Toastmasters #1272692
Elinora_Reynolds@hotmail.com

New Matters . . .

"Me, evaluate him? How can I? I've only been a Toastmaster a few months and he's been here forever! He's so good, and I don't know anything."

Thomas, the newest member of the club, struggled to fill in the form without the pen shaking. He focused on every word Dave said. He searched every movement and every word for anything Dave could improve. He knew he had to find something. Then Thomas heard it.

"Oops, I shouldn't ah said that."

Thomas could talk about grammar and apologizing.

Dave finished his speech and sat down. Thomas scribbled as fast as he could.

When he was called on to give his evaluation of Dave's speech, Thomas carefully obeyed all the rules he'd been taught. He praised Dave for his speaking ability. Then he took a deep breath.

"Dave, there is one small way I think you can improve. You had one, short sentence when you apologized for what you said and when you did, your grammar sounded lazy; not up to your usual standard. I encourage you to work on this as you continue your good work." After the meeting, Thomas started shaking when Dave came up to him. He was afraid he had made a mistake in his evaluation.

"Thanks, Thomas, I didn't realize I slipped like that. Thanks for noticing and pointing it out." Thomas' chest swelled. He went to work that day with more self-confidence than he had felt for days.

Dave went to work and gave a presentation to the company president constantly thinking of his word choice.

That night, Thomas met with his Toastmaster mentor.

"How are you doing, Thomas? Did you enjoy being an evaluator for the first time?"

"Yes, it was great. Dave said I helped him be a better speaker and I learned to listen really hard. I know even my opinion counts."

Ladies and gentlemen, as I welcome you as new members of Toastmasters, I tell you this story because I hope each of you will know how important you are, how important your opinion is. I want each of you to know that you know more about speaking and evaluating than you think you know. You listen to speakers every day in dozens of situations. You speak dozens, if not hundreds of times a day. What Toastmasters offers you is help enhancing, strengthening and expanding the skills you already have. We promise to give you all the help we can. We promise to give you honest and open support through teaching and evaluation.

What we ask from you is your honesty when you are evaluating your fellow members. We encourage your questions. Because you don't know us well and have not heard us speak many times before, you have fresh ears which can give us a multitude of insights. Thank you for joining us. We welcome you.

J. Christine Richards
Castle Rock Toastmasters #3680
passingthequill@gmail.com

The Pen . . .

I was born in Fort Worth, Texas, a son to a single mother named Mary. Ever since I can remember, my mother has always been a great source of strength and inspiration for me. Despite the challenges that life presented her, she always found ways to overcome and persevere. Although I did not have a traditional father in my everyday life, my mother always ensured I learned the lessons that I needed. Father figures for me were my grandfather, my godfather, and my mother's only brother. Still, some of the most important lessons I learned were from my mother. She did not finish high school yet was always employed. She did not have her driver's license and, as one can imagine, we never had our own vehicle, yet we never struggled to find our way around. No matter what, my mom always found ways to make ends meet, and always found a strength from within that never let her give up. She never let down. I can still hear her say, "you gotta keep on going; it's too easy to quit!"

Perhaps my most memorable times with my mom were the early mornings. My mom would wake up early enough each morning to make breakfast tacos that she would sell at work to her co-workers. Since we did not have a car, we relied on the city bus system. We lived in an apartment on the southeast side of Austin, Texas, and the nearest bus stop was roughly 6 blocks away. While not a long distance, the start of this trek began with a huge hill that spanned two blocks, and it was steep. It might have well been a mountain (though I had never yet seen a mountain to compare it with). Each day we would begin this trek, and being overly dramatic as kids can sometimes be, I would begin each climb with complaints and a sigh.

One day in particular I remember with pristine clarity was the day that inspires me the most. I remember this day as being a cloudy but sunny fall day. As is normal in the early fall in Texas, it was a bit humid, and for whatever reason I especially did not look forward to our morning ritual. The day had worn on me so much already that not even half way up the hill I had to ask my mom for some help.

So there we were: my mom with her purse over her shoulder, carrying a bag full of tacos and a second bag with her lunch -- yet it was I who needed help. You see, I had what seemed to me at the time to be the most bulky, heavy, and painfully uncomfortable pen to carry in all the world. There was no way I was going to make it up that hill, not carrying this heavy load. And so I asked, I begged, and I pleaded with her to please carry my pen for me so that I could make it up that hill. My mother took my pen and placed it in her purse, and now aggressively urged me to get up that hill and to stop complaining. Having been relieved of this huge burden I was able to carry on.

It wasn't until we arrived at the bus stop that my mom took a moment to speak to me about the help she gave me. She looked me in the eye and said, "Here is your pen. You see it was just a pen and it wasn't that heavy." She said, "Sometimes in life the things that seem the most difficult are really not, once you take a moment to look at them." She then said, "Now tomorrow, you will carry your pen because it is your responsibility and I won't always be around to carry it for you. Sometimes, you just gotta keep on going!"

The next day would come, and I would carry my pen, and would do so for every day after that at least as far as I can remember. However, I never forgot that lesson. Today, I serve in the United States Air Force and I have done so for nearly 17 years. Each day I wake up, get ready, and put on my uniform. However, right before I step out the door I make sure that I have my keys, my wallet, and -- more importantly -- I make sure that I have my pen. I always make sure that I have my pen, because it is my responsibility to carry my pen now. And, each day it makes me think of those things that my mother spoke to me about that long-ago day -- that things could always be worse, and that if I take a moment and pause, I just may realize that things aren't as tough as they may first seem.

James P. Seballes
Defenders of Speech Toastmasters #897557
seballes@me.com

My Best Friend. . .

My name is Margaret Anne Seyer, and I was born and raised in Queens, New York. Because New York, also known as "the Big Apple," is a highly populous state, people are always coming and going due to all of our popular attractions. In light of all of the natives, newcomers and visitors who enjoy our great state, I am happily intrigued that many have not forgotten one of God's most special creations in the whole wide world – the dog.

Have you ever wondered what our dogs must think of us? I once heard that the reason the dog has so many friends is that he always wags his tail more than his tongue. It goes without saying that everything I need to know, I learned from my dog (and best friend), Larry. When I come home from a hard day's work, Larry is the first one to greet me. I frequently receive kisses daily – for no particular reason. Because he has proven time and time again that he can love unconditionally, he extends this love to my parents and siblings because after all, they're part of his family, too! Good-natured and very intelligent, Larry always seems to know when my mom or grandmother calls, and gives them a cute message over the phone in doggie language that they, of course, understand. When I'm sad or angry, my buddy consoles me in his own way and, unlike a doctor or counselor, there is no charge for his special love and attention. Like any smart creature, Larry will never pass up the opportunity to go for a joy ride in the car, receive a tasty snack or a gentle atta-boy pat on the back.

Imagine being out and about town and someone you could not hear or see was suddenly approaching you. Before potential harm could ever happen, your friend and personal bodyguard instinctively hears and sees them, and they are stopped in their tracks before anything happens. When I come home from work, my friend, without saying a word, tells me that he is glad to see me and is ready for our daily walk. No matter what is going on in my life, Larry, amazingly, knows just how to put a smile on my face and make me feel better. I remember Mom reminding me to surround myself with special friends and good people who are intelligent, passionate, God-fearing and always the same kind-hearted person who does not judge me by my looks but by my heart. Guess what? My loving and compassionate friend, Larry has all of those qualities!

In addition to becoming the best public speaker and leader that I am capable of, my goal in life is to be as good a person as my dog already thinks I am. Because God created the dog, I believe that he is man's (and woman's) best friend. Larry, for sure, is *my* best friend. If you are a dog owner, perhaps you will agree with the heartfelt words of American wildlife photographer, writer and wildlife preservationist, Roger Caras, who once said "Dogs are not our whole life, but they make our lives whole."

Toastmasters and friends, if you are in need of a true and devoted friend who will love and accept you JUST as you are, why not consider a D.O.G. (who Depends On God) for all of his wants and needs. Because they give us unqualified love for their entire life, I believe that dogs are a gift from God. I don't know about you but, "if there are no dogs in heaven, then when I die, I want to go where they went." (Will Rogers)

If you think you see tears on this page, well, it's probably so. . .

Margaret Seyer, CC
Simply Speaking Toastmasters #677476
backhometoast@yahoo.com

Happy New Year . . .

This year, I wish for you special gifts from God alone. Our Father God loves you even in your darkest hour when you've cried and moaned.

First, I wish for you *strength* – the strength to stand for a just purpose and the strength to keep you steady. I also wish for you *patience* – the patience of Job. Don't move until God is ready!

This year, I wish for you *wisdom* – the wisdom to know when to move on faith and when to leave well enough alone. I also wish for you *courage* – the courage to take all of your requests through prayer to God's throne.

This year, I wish for you *love* – nothing is more powerful than love; for we are a direct product of God's heart.

And I also wish for you *faith* – the faith of just a mustard seed to believe that light defeats the dark.

This year, I wish for you *joy* in abundance to brighten your day.

And I also wish for you the *power of prayer* – I offer you the prayer of our ancestors to keep our family safe and sound in every way.

This year, I've packaged your gifts in *sincerity* including *respect, dignity, integrity* and *ambition.* As I offer you this food for thought, the light of the truth and my blessing for a long, healthy and prosperous life, I've asked God to give you *direction, motivation, understanding* and *passion.*

I now give you permission to take my dreams and pursue them for yourself as you reach for that glass ceiling while refusing to put your hopes and desires back on the shelf.

Last year, I stuffed your stocking with my blood, sweat and tears because I've seen you all alone, but that's because I can't give you redemption. You must achieve that on your own.

Finally this year, I give you enough to change the world where you stand, because next year, the future of our world will be placed back in your hands.

Happy New Year!

Roy L. Shankle, CC
Absolutely Articulate Toastmasters #1272692
cam-tre@hotmail.com

Got Opportunity?

Sometimes we are walking along not thinking about anything in particular and – BANG! -- opportunity presents itself. The sad thing is that all too often we do not hear it, or see it, or feel it.

I have been trying to get started on a project for about four months. Each day I find a new way of avoiding it. There is so much to do that I simply do not find the time.

Well today opportunity presented itself and I listened, I saw, I felt. I heard a friend talking about his success in the area of my project. I saw that the time to start was *now*. I felt that I actually was worthy of completing my project. Bang! I started to write my book.

Now I know that I can accomplish my goals and achieve my dream.

What happened? Two things:

I listened to myself. Yes it really can be that easy. Opportunity lives within each of us throughout each day of our lives. When we listen to the best that is within us, we hear the "small still voice" and it is wisdom, power and right.

I started. You see that voice told me that nothing ever gets finished unless it actually gets started. I know that is so obvious, and yet how often do we not start simply because we do not know how things will turn out?

I bet there is an opportunity you want to pursue. Please listen to your inner voice. Please start. You will be glad you did. The world will be a better place because you did.

Ron Shuster
WryToast Toastmasters #8358
rmshus@comcast.net

Teach . . .

Teach somebody something.
If you can read, thank a teacher.
If you can write, thank a teacher.
If you can sing, thank a teacher.
If you can act, thank a teacher.
If you are a lifelong learner, thank a teacher.
If you are a teacher, thank a teacher.
Now teach somebody something, too!

"Best teachers seldom teach - they just be."
–Haki Madhubuti

Annette Sills-Brown
Absolutely Articulate Toastmasters #1272692
annette_sills-brown@dpsk12.org

A Love Letter . . .

June 14, 2011

Dear Sierra,

My child, this is my love letter to you. You are a precious miracle and a gift from God.

My child, your name, "Sierra Channelle," means a long rugged mountain chain with a channel of water running through it which is symbolic of our journey together. We've experienced highs and lows; but like flowing water we've stayed the course. Life is molding, shaping and strengthening us as we strive to embrace change and grow wiser from life's lessons.

My child, motherhood has given me a purpose and the knowledge of what it means to transcend self. Being a mother has taught me so much about myself and the true meaning of life, which are the fruits of the spirit: love, joy, peace, long-suffering, gentleness, faith, meekness and temperance.

My child, you are a beautiful young lady, and God has blessed you with many gifts and talents. You have the ability to achieve exceedingly abundantly above and beyond your greatest imagination, My hope is that you will always put God first in your life.

My child, you are a leader, so have faith and know that if you apply yourself and work hard, you will reap the fruits of your labor. Know your purpose, and your worth; love yourself; and never settle for less than your very best. I've pressed you toward your authentic self, so, my child, be free and reach for the mountains and soar with the eagles. Be who you are meant to be.

My child, at times I have faltered and fallen short of the mark, but, as I have, remember to always get back up. With every fiber of my being, I have made an effort to be your nurturer, your care taker, your mentor, your inspirer, your disciplinarian and your best friend.

My child, I leave you with my eternal love and legacy for you to share with the generations to come.

Warmest love,

Mom

Pamela Y. Simmons
Absolutely Articulate Toastmasters #1272692
enlighten_pya@msn.com

I Am What I Am . . .

I am a daughter, big sister, cousin, niece, granddaughter and a friend.
I am what I am.

I am a true blue African American born in 1995.

I am a historian, a student, a mathematician.
I am what I am.

I am a cook and a drama queen.
I am what I am.

I am a pianist.
I am what I am.

I am a person who is blessed with a home and family by God.

This is who I am and you can't change me.
I am what I am.

I am what I am.

Sierra C. Simmons (age 16)
Daughter of Absolutely Articulate Toastmasters Member #1272692
enlighten_pya@msn.com

A "Gluten" for Punishment . . .

I was recently in a King Soopers grocery store buying a card, when I heard a boy ask, "Mom, what does that sign mean ...that doesn't have wheat in it?" His mother was cross, "No, it means it's gluten free!" They went on. I stopped. They were both right, actually. I was so glad to hear that gluten free is catching on, and people, even in the grocery store, are talking about it.

What is gluten? Gluten is a protein that occurs in grains like wheat, rye and barley. That's why the gluten free symbol is usually shown with a few shafts of wheat with a line through it. Gluten is the part of the grain that is sticky and starchy. It's what makes your pizza crust chewy, and what holds the cookie together.

Unfortunately, about one in 130 people has celiac disease. Celiac disease is an autoimmune response that causes damage to the small intestine. A person with celiac disease can't digest any grain containing gluten. Today I learned that May is celiac awareness month.

Since gluten affects the small intestine, the list of symptoms for celiac disease sounds a lot like the commercial for Pepto-Bismol: nausea, heartburn, indigestion, upset stomach and diarrhea

In fact the list of symptoms is about 300 items long. There is even a list of *atypical* symptoms. So, instead of diarrhea, these people get constipated. Classic symptoms include weight loss, abdominal distention, flatulence, frequent bulky, foul-smelling stools. Celiac disease is not rare; it is just under-diagnosed.

Atypical symptoms include bone pain, anemia (which I have), ataxia, dental enamel defects, brain fog, fatigue, irritability, weakness, weight gain, constipation, intensely itchy and burning rash, depression and peripheral neuropathy.

Because I was having a lot of these symptoms, I decided to try the gluten-free diet. It was several months before I could tell a difference, and I thought I would die. Think about it: No pizza, no donuts, no pasta and no bread! You would be surprised at the number of things that gluten is added to that supposedly makes some food taste better. After compiling a comprehensive list of food items that have gluten, I've decided that it appears to be just about *everything*!

When I went to my grandmother's birthday, I found myself cheating a little bit on my new gluten-free diet. It took about three weeks for my system to finally start to get over the "two bites" of bread and cake that I had eaten at her party. Wow!

Actually, there are a lot of processed foods that are specifically made to be gluten-free, and most unprocessed foods are naturally gluten free. I feel so much better now that I am healthy, and guess what? I finally don't miss at all what I've been missing. Friends, I am happy to report that now that I know what I am missing, I am no longer a "gluten" for punishment.

Abigail Smucker
Simply Speaking Toastmasters #677476
abigail_smucker@yahoo.com

Second Chance. . .

George lay in his bed in the hospital, suffering from a failing heart and the ravages of cancer. He was shrunken, the illness slowly taking its toll. He knew he didn't have long to live. But he had stayed alive much longer than anyone expected. Why? Because he wanted a second chance. Now his son, Alan, opened the hospital door, and walked into the room. Alan had been in Germany for three long years, serving with the U.S. Army. George sent audio tapes to Alan to keep in contact over those three years. Now his second and probably last chance had arrived. George said, "I love you, son." It was a risk for George because he had never said that before to Alan, although he acted in loving ways. Alan replied, "I love you too, Dad." George hugged him and weakly said, "Come back when you can." Three days later, George died, his heart at peace, having used his second chance.

How many of us wish we had a second chance in a relationship, in a job, with a family member, with a daughter or son, even with the wife's cat that we are not too sure about? How many of us rush past the opportunity to treasure the holy moments or spiritual connection between two human beings because we are too busy? Each of us is here on Earth for a very short time. If we are lucky, we may get a second chance to refocus on those moments when our souls touch. Will we have the courage it takes when our second chance comes? Will we be able to do something totally different from our past life pattern? Although my Dad died in November, 1972, I miss him terribly. At his funeral, I found out he bragged about me all the time - a demonstration of his love. I still feel his spirit, his love of life and the people who are with me today.

Second chances... I think about Vietnam, the hot shrapnel dropping around me at the Quin Nohn Ammo Depot, the helicopter which lost its hydraulics but landed safely, the man shooting at me, while I was sitting in the helicopter door. For whatever reason, I survived and was granted the second chance that 58,000 young men missed. I have two wonderful children, Dustin and Roxanna, as a result of my second chance.

I worked for 25 years with 4-H youth and wanted to change the world. Then Katie (my 12 year old babysitter) accidentally shot and killed her nine year old sister and wounded her mother. Katie was in youth detention for five years. God told me I could make a difference so I wrote letters to her for five years. What if I hadn't used that chance or had been judgmental or too afraid of saying the wrong thing? She says she would have committed suicide if I hadn't written those letters of support. I learned that I didn't have to change the whole world, but I could make a difference in one person's life. Because I wasn't judgmental like so many others, I gave Katie a second chance.

I was divorced in 1991, and my daughter, Roxanna directed her anger at me. It ripped my heart out because I love her so much. Her Dad had broken her heart. As the anger subsided after several years, I was determined to create a second chance by going on trips, cooking together, having coffee with her, attending her fashion shows and even letting Xorussi (her pit bull) crawl in my sleeping bag with me while at Roxanna's home.

What does it take to create a second chance? It takes humility to admit you screwed up, and it is hard work. It takes willingness to change, it takes patience and lots of unconditional love... and yet it may not work out. You may not even get the chance to finish it as life is very unpredictable. But don't lose hope - never lose hope. Because we never know until we try. I close with a note I received from my daughter, Roxanna that makes me cry:

Dearest Dad, You are the rising sun for many people. You bring laughter when people are down. You bring comfort to those in pain. If your mission in life is to reach out to those in need of love, you have succeeded. I am honored to even know someone like you. I am blessed to have you as my Dad. I wouldn't be the confident, capable and emotionally strong person that I am without you. Thank you for all of your love and support from me and the many others who make it through the day because of you. Love, Roxanna

This note makes me feel very humble and loved. It is worth more than anything. I am honored to be her Dad.

Second chances are a risk and an opportunity. Take a moment right now and look at your own life. What second chance do you long for that would give your heart peace? Is it a friend or a family member? Maybe someone you need to make amends with -- remember we are only here a short time; some of us much shorter than others. Do not wait until you are on your deathbed. Do not wait until it is too late. Your second chance is waiting on you, right now.

Alan Swartz
Double Talk Toastmasters #4444
alanpaulswartz@aol.com

My Father Taught Me Numbers. . .

How, you ask? Was he an educator? Was he in politics? Well, the last thing you would think about him was that he was a gangster...yes, a gangster...for real!

I am a "numbers" person who generally has a harder time remembering names rather than a number due largely to my beloved Father.

I remember sitting by the side of his bed, "studying" the dogs for the dog track; carefully assessing the numbers assigned to the best and worst dogs. Watching the smoke from his Viceroy cigarettes floating curled and purple up into the air, Dad would say, "Spooky Mae, come grade these dogs." I learned the importance of an "A" dog versus a "C" dog and I truly believe that this helped me to realize that being the best was important in life. Daddy would let me pick out my own dog and he would even place a $2 bet for me. I remember the nights waiting up to see if I won. Often, I would go to sleep waiting for Daddy because he wouldn't come home 'til morning.

My mother never smoked; but one of the ways I knew that she truly loved my father ("Thomas" she called him), was the way she took his Viceroy, put it between her delicately rouged lips, and light his cigarette without taking a puff. She would hand it to him by putting it in his mouth while driving. While words were never said, the love was there.

My mother worked tirelessly as an awesome cook in the best Denver hotels - remember the "Cosmo" and "Brown Palace"? My mother would stand on her legs more than 16 hours a day to ensure that my sister and I had a better life. She was the favorite cook of President Johnson when he came to town. Meanwhile, my grandmother raised us while my parents were gone.

As I got older and more "grown," I found evidence of who Daddy really was. Often I would go out with people I had no business with and nothing would ever happen to me. Once, I even popped up at a craps game and had an unfortunate meeting with my Father. Oops! After that, more people knew that I was "Thomas's daughter."

Little did I know that I was always protected – my father was known as "Thomas" to the outside world and a handsome gangster.

Who knew that in later years, I would grow up to be a banker, working statistical analysis of training data, a senior tax preparer and a realtor?

Although my father taught me numbers, my Heavenly Father taught me a foundation for my life!

Vanessa Thomas-Jones
Absolutely Articulate Toastmasters #1272692
v.thomas-jones@comcast.net

Single Fatherhood. . .

In 2004, I became a single father to a daughter age eleven and a son age four. In spite of the ups and downs that come with parenting, I have thoroughly enjoyed being a single father.

When I was about 28, I remember my grandmother asking me when I was going to give her some great-grandbabies. Keep in mind that my grandmother (whom we affectionately called "Dear") was blessed to have seven children of her own. In addition, all but one of Dear's seven children brought one to thirteen children into the world. Whew! When Grandmother asked me that question, it wasn't like she didn't already have a bunch of great-grandchildren – because she did. For example, my sister's son just had a little girl. I responded to Dear's inquiry by explaining, "I do want children, Dear, but I just don't want to get married." As you read on, you'll see that I was right!

By the time I had turned 45 years old, I found myself twice-divorced and a single dad of a daughter (from my first marriage) and a son (from my second). I honestly never dreamed that my life would end up being married and divorced twice. As a mentor of young men, I now tell them

"Your life is based on choices that you make. They all come with consequences – good or bad. So learn by listening to my personal story about the choices that I elected to make and hear of the consequences that came as a result of my actions."

As a single dad, I found myself faced with lots of challenges. Things like getting my children enrolled in school, taking care of the numerous vaccinations that are required by law, making sure my daughter's hair was done, engaging in after-school activities, dating (oh my God!), dealing with their mom, and providing everything else they needed, from A through Z, that is not mentioned in any parenting books.

The problems that I experienced with the mothers of my children are too numerous to mention. No matter how hard I tried to treat them with courtesy, respect and even ensure that my conversations about them with our kids was positive and constructive, they still many times made my job as a single dad rough and hard to swallow. However, for the sake of our children, whom I love dearly, I have tried to remain positive.

As a result of the personal choices made throughout my life, the following are some of the things that I experienced after becoming a parent: I was removed from my job and taken to jail in handcuffs because I told my first wife that I would kill her if she didn't leave me alone. Although I did not mean this *literally* (because I am just not that kind of a person), I allowed myself to be pushed to the limit when I made that stupid statement. As a result of a thoughtless statement that came out of my mouth, it cost me one night in jail, anger management classes at $30.00 dollars per class, court costs and one year probation . . . and that was just one incident! The funny thing about this particular story is in spite of the fact that I left her, she made the courts think that I was the one trying to get her back. Not on your life!

Meanwhile my second divorce was a less stressful one as we worked on the divorce together. Although we agreed to split visitation with my son 50/50, I ended up with him every day (except for weekends) due to Mom's alcohol abuse problem. At the beginning of last year, we finally got back on our 50/50 arrangement that now allows my son more time to spend with his mother. While the courts ordered child support to be paid to me, I never received a dime. Needless to say, had the shoe been on the other foot, I would have been ordered to jail a long time before now.

In spite of all that I have gone through, I feel happy and blessed to be Dad to my beloved children and to have them in my life. Yes, I have gone through a number of challenging hurdles; however, it is clear that had I made smarter choices, I would not have suffered so many scars and blunders. Friends, when it is all said and done, I consider myself the "winner" because I am the father of two beautiful kids that I love dearly. In addition to the great relationship that God has blessed me to have with my stepdaughter, I also have been blessed to mentor a young man the same age as my son, to share my life experiences with him while encouraging him to be careful what he does and says – as it all matters in the game of life.

Today when people ask me how many children I have, I happily say, "four."

Mike Thompson
Absolutely Articulate Toastmaster #1272692
mike@thefathershowrp.org

Sometimes, Things Happen for a Reason. . .

There is a lot of truth to the saying that when life throws you lemons, make lemonade! I was laid off in February, 2009. My cousin was losing his business, and my Father was disappointed; he was turning 75 that same year.

While pondering world hunger, my cousin woke up at 3:00 AM with the idea of Eleanor's Garden – a tool to help the world feed itself. My dad came to Denver for his 75th birthday party about a month later. By chance, my cousin called my Dad and we ended up talking about his garden dream. The layoff, the dream and the birthday phone call that connected me with my cousin have turned into a wonderful partnership with lofty humanitarian goals.

What makes Eleanor's Garden so special is that it won the "Green Thumb Award" for the best new garden product even before it came to market. The core idea of providing a practical way for people of all ages, backgrounds and abilities to grow their own fresh and healthy vegetables caught the interest of many! The garden in a kit is complete, compact, lightweight and portable. The elderly, who can no longer enjoy their row gardens, can set up an

Eleanor's Garden in less than an hour. People with disabilities can garden from their wheelchairs. School children can learn how to grow and prepare healthy food. People in apartments can have a garden on their balcony. Eleanor's Garden provides opportunities for everyone!

The garden tubs are made with recyclable plastic, coconut-peat drainage mats and coco-peat growing medium. There is no need to use traditional peat moss which is a mined, non-renewable resource. There is no need to ship heavy soil. The seeds are organic. Eleanor's Garden makes it simple and easy for anyone, anywhere to experience the joy of gardening – just add water!

A year and a half after the idea sprouted, I am happy to report that Eleanor's Garden is entering the marketplace this spring. The first units will be rolled out by the First Lady and Governor of Montana, who are doing a pilot program using Eleanor's Garden for their Montana school gardening initiative. More units will be used in Vancouver and, hopefully, the trend will catch on in school districts all across the USA and Canada. The timing couldn't be better. Eleanor's Garden is named after Eleanor Roosevelt, who planted a Victory Garden on the White House lawn. First Lady Michelle Obama also planted a garden and has a very proactive healthy living and exercise agenda. In addition, large retailers, garden centers, garden writers, television and radio hosts, extension agents, green bloggers and many others have expressed interest in selling and helping our company gain exposure in the marketplace.

Eleanor's Garden's original goal - providing the world a tool to help feed itself - is still in our sights. Depending on the success of the commercial side of the garden, we plan to establish the Eleanor's Garden Foundation to help people in need through the Eleanor's Garden Foundation. Needless to say, my Toastmasters leadership and communication training have helped me to step up, speak out and blossom into an entrepreneur who aspires to positively change the world one seed at a time.

Heidi Williams, CC
(Co-Founder – Eleanor's Garden, LLC)
Simply Speaking Toastmasters #677476
Absolutely Articulate Toastmasters #1272692
hwilliamswd@msn.com

Never Give Up. . .

On August 21, 2010, my best friend and beloved dog of sixteen years lost the ability to walk. The arthritis at the base of his spine had progressed to the point that his fully functional back legs became useless appendages. The sadness and confusion in his dark, brown eyes punctuated his lack of understanding. This used to work; why doesn't this work anymore?

The veterinarian talked about "options." None of them were acceptable to me. I brought my paralyzed best friend home and refused to shed a single tear. After all, it was he who had been a source of strength since I was a scared little boy. He had taken care of me when all others abused, brutalized and abandoned me. He had earned more than I could ever repay, but I would still try.

After three acupuncture sessions, we knew that he would never walk again. Nor would he ever chase a rabbit, never bound up to me at the end of a long day, never even stand up to see what made a strange noise.

I didn't give up. I refused to. If the roles had been reversed, Max would never let the idea of defeat enter into his mind. You can learn a lot from a being that has such courage and kindness.

Max rolls around in a wheelchair now. Every single morning, he barks with barely restrained jubilation until I get him into his new magic carpet. His ears flap in a breeze that he himself creates. He doesn't walk anymore. He runs! He sprints! He flies!

Neighbors come out to offer their condolences to me about Max. However, after seeing him move, after seeing that the only breaks necessary are the ones that I need, they change their mind. They want to apologize to him because the old man (that's me) can't keep up.

Never give up on faith. Never give up on hope. Never give up on those you love. In the darkest hours, they will shine a light and surprise you with miracles.

Like a dog that can't walk . . . but can outrun you!

Tyler Withrow
Gates to Excellence Toastmasters #3413
twithrow@cowest.com

Nature Guides Us. . .

When we feel sad, conflicted, lost, alone, Mother Nature comforts us. Think about this — on a cloudy or foggy or snowy day, one can't see the sun — it's obscured. We think it's gone. But in reality, it is there all the time. And it will shine for us again soon. So it is with our problems — the Light is always there behind the events, and it will definitely shine again. We just need to have faith, looking for the Light behind the clouds.

With thunder storms comes the rainbow. One can always look for the rainbow in the storms of our life — believe that it is there and it will manifest.

When we see the beautiful trees in the forest or woods or mountains, remember that each magnificent, individual tree came from one tiny little seed -- and each tree is unique and different. So too, each one of us came from one tiny individual seed and we are each unique — no two people, no matter how crowded our space, are alike. No one can replace you — no one has the unique gifts that you have. Just like the trees, we must flourish and offer whatever unique gifts we have to the Universe—or there will be something beautiful missing.

We know from quantum physics that each one of us is a unique field of energy, and energy cannot be destroyed. We come from the Supreme Source of energy and we return there. We are like waves in the ocean — we roll along as our own force of being, and then eventually we return and are lost in the embrace of the ocean. We are all One. We are never alone or separate, no matter how much it may feel that way at times.

Nature is our great teacher, our comforter, our inspiration. We are grateful that we can look to Nature for the guidance we need to be happy and to grow.

Diane Woods
Aurorators Toastmasters #2136
diawoods@comcast.net

The "Whole Truth" Seeker . . .

"I swear to tell the truth, the whole truth, and nothing but the truth, so help me God." The year was 1972; she was 17 years old and the first of eight children to leave home to attend college. As she left her family and beloved church, she vowed to find a church home while attending college and to join that church under "watch care."

During the first month of school, she'd walk down the campus hill into the town of Canton, Missouri, alone to attend church. There she found a church home, Second Baptist Church, which met on the first and third Sundays of the month because the itinerant minister also pastored a church in LaGrange, Missouri, a few miles down the road, on the second and fourth Sundays of the month.

It was here that she met an elderly couple, Deacon Willard and Ida Jackson. Ida Jackson worked in the cafeteria with the student at the campus and told her when the church met. Deacon Jackson also served as a Sunday school teacher. He was a gentle giant. His body bowed forward on two metal hand canes under the oppression of polio. Deacon Jackson often quoted a favorite scripture at the end of the Sunday school lesson and challenged the student to learn it. She did! She returned two weeks later and proudly recited, "Philippians 4:8 Finally, brethren, whatsoever things are true, whatsoever thing are honest, whatsoever things are just, whatsoever things are pure, whatsoever things are lovely, if there be any virtue, and if there be any praise, think on these things."

Deacon Jackson of course was very proud of the student and nicknamed her "Sunshine." Little did she know the impact of this scriptural deposit in her life. The student quickly learned that as difficulties, struggles, joys or sorrows filled her life, this verse Philippians 4:8 would be a "whole truth seeker."

What do you mean, "Whole truth seeker"? The student would line up life situations to this verse to determine the "truth" or "falsehood" of the situation. For instance, in time of discouragement or fear, she'd speak Philippians 4:8 aloud and seek the truth of God's word regarding discouragement and fear. The student, now a woman, would say aloud, "Why be downcast oh my soul, put your trust in God," or "God has not given me a spirit of fear, but power, love, and a sound mind." Years later, she married and gave birth to two children. She sought the "whole truth seeker" verse regarding child rearing and remembered the promise of God. "Train up a child in the way that he should go and when he is old, he will not depart from it."

Yes, this woman is convinced Philippians 4:8 is the "whole truth seeker." She confidently rests in the assurance that God has thoughts of peace, not evil, toward her with an expected end to give her a future and a hope. She was once young and is now much older, she has never seen the righteous forsaken nor the seed of God begging for bread.

And she will live a prosperous, long and satisfied life, because she found the "whole truth seeker" in Philippians 4:8.

Frances Woolery-Jones
Absolutely Articulate Toastmasters #1272692
franceswjones@comcast.net

The Story of Collecting the Sunlight. . .

I still remember vividly the story my mom told us when I was in elementary school. It was during the rainy season preceding the summer in Shanghai. My siblings and I were so bored because we could rarely play outside. We missed the sun, the fresh air and the smell of the flowers and grass. There was nothing to do when the weather was like that.

It was a Sunday afternoon. We were playing with building blocks on a bamboo mat on the floor. One of my older sisters had already fallen asleep next to me. Mom walked in with a plate of fresh fruits; we all became excited because it was snack and story time.

Mom sat down on the same mat with us. She looked at the window. It was completely covered by the heavy rain like a huge waterfall painting. Mom's eyes glowed as she moved a little closer to us and started the story. That was one of those stories that I would remember forever...

A long, long time ago, there was a family of mice living in a beautiful field right at the edge of a tall mountain. It was the end of summer so the mouse family started preparing for the winter.

Every mouse was working hard gathering nuts, paddy and other food so there would be enough for everyone when winter came. There was one mouse that didn't seem to be collecting anything. He was running around from tree to tree, flower to flower, rock to rock and hill to hill. Sometimes he would sit on a rock next to the mountain stream listening to the gurgling sound of water.

One of the mice asked, "What are you doing Frankie? Why are you not collecting anything?"

"I am working. I am collecting things for the winter." Frankie replied.

"What are you collecting?"

"I am collecting the sunlight."

"What?" The other mice were confused and thought it was a joke. They laughed.

Frankie didn't say anything but continued working.

The winter finally arrived. The weather became colder and colder. The mouse family stayed inside the caves and did not worry about the food. One day, the other mice went to Frankie's cave and asked, "Frankie, what are you going to do for the winter? Where are the things you have collected?" Frankie smiled and said, "Please close your eyes everyone."

All the mice were confused but still closed their eyes.

"Here is my first collection. This is the sunlight I had collected from the summer. Can you see the bright sun light now?" He continued.

Suddenly, the dim cave turned bright. The mice started feeling warm as if they were in the summer sunshine.

"What else did you collect?" The mice asked.

Frankie started to describe the red, pink, purple flowers, the green leaves, grasses and the golden paddies. He described everything vividly. All the mice could see the summer color of the field, the mountain, the brooks and the flowers.

"Anything else, Frankie?" The mice were very excited and wanted more.

Frankie recited a poem. He also told a beautiful story. Everyone was fascinated and touched by his story and poem. They started going to Frankie's room every day.

The winter passed by quickly without anyone noticing.

Collecting the sunlight! To me, going to Toastmasters is like collecting the sunlight. Everyone's speech is a ray of sunlight because I can always learn and be inspired from everyone's speech.

We are living in a fast-paced world. Everyone is bustling on the road of life. Everyone is trying to maximize his or her material wealth. Please don't forget to pause and take a moment to nurture your spirit and your love of life. I call it *sunlight*. To me, a strong spirit is more important than material wealth.

Shelley Xiao
Solar Speaker Toastmasters #9548
xiao_shelley@yahoo.com

Contributors

Connie Akins: Connie Akins considers herself most fortunate to be a member in the "family" of the Simply Speaking Toastmasters club #677476 of Aurora, Colorado. She is also a member of the Excelsior Advanced Toastmaster Club #3247 of Lakewood, Colorado. In addition to her outstanding work in leadership as past VP-Membership for the Simply Speaking Club, Connie is looking forward to her new job as secretary for District 26 for the 2011-2012 term. Connie loves to use words to inspire people; she also loves to compete. As the owner of an army of little trophies from past Toastmaster contests, she is most proud of winning First Place in Evaluation at the District level. But Connie's real passion is using Healing Journaling, which she created, and her own original piano music to help people heal their emotional wounds and begin living their dreams. She has started her own business called *Chrysalis Touch* through which she speaks, facilitates workshops and hosts private concerts. She is also writing a book about Healing Journaling called "Ray of Hope." Connie graduated from San Diego State University with a degree in Creative Writing and partially completed a Masters degree in Counseling from Denver Seminary. She is the proud mama hen of four children and is happily married to Alan Swartz, past District Governor with whom she goes to a lot of movies and Toastmasters events! She also makes the best salsa ever. Her number one hobby is having fun.

Shankara Gil Antero: Gil Antero currently serves as past president of the Absolutely Articulate #1272692 Club, a president's distinguished Toastmasters Club located in Aurora, Colorado. Having earned his Competent Communicator Award, he has participated in a number of Toastmasters International Speech and Table Topics Contests. In 2010, he won first place in both the speech and table topics competition categories when representing the Aurorators Toastmasters Club #2136. Gil has worked as a clinical massage therapist for more than twelve years, and is currently associated with Vitality Health Center, a pain and decompression clinic in Denver, Colorado. Born and raised in Harlem, New York, he spent four memorable years as a child with his beloved grandmother in Cuba. Gil's mother, an educator and prolific poet, made sure that Gil went to school every day even after he came home from school. Gil is currently on the Board of Directors with Sankofa Wholistic Healthcare Group that represents African American healthcare practitioners dedicated to educating the African American and Afro Latino communities about how to maintain better health. Gil studied massage therapy for three years and upon graduation, he completed a one year internship in a nonsurgical, orthopedic clinic. He is currently working on an innovative project called "Wheels of Wellness" that will bring the concept of wholistic wellness to communities anywhere a car can travel to. Gil is single, with two adult children and two teenage grandsons. His hobbies include architectural construction, scuba diving and volunteer work in his community. Phone number and email removed – basic safety.

Cybele Antonow: Cybele Antonow is a dual member of the Simply Speaking Toastmasters Club #667476 and Aurorators Club #2136 both located in Aurora, Colorado. She has served in a number of officer roles including Sergeant-At-Arms, Secretary and VP of Education. Having competed in both the International Humorous Speech Contest and the International Speech & Table Topics Contest (both at the club and area levels), she earned first place in the Aurorators Club. As an active member of the Simply Speaking mentoring program, she enjoys helping others to help them achieve their goals. Cybele has worked as a Radiologic Technologist for twenty-five years, and recently returned to college to earn her Bachelor's degree in Speech Communication while earning her teaching licensure. While volunteering at public schools, she takes pride in supporting teachers and especially students to learn and grow. Having recently started her own business, Cybele strives to create a team of leaders who share her proactive mindset as she proudly brings skincare and spa-quality products into the home of interested consumers. Mrs. Antonow has been married for 8 years and is the mother of one beautiful daughter, Sheridan, age 14. Cybele's hobbies include scrapbooking, photography, cooking and travel. She is a devoted member of the Smoky Hill Vineyard Church and regularly attends bible study courses while also serving as a volunteer with childcare and families in need.

Shirley J. Armstrong: Shirley Armstrong is a charter member of the Absolutely Articulate Toastmaster Club #1272692 located in Aurora, Colorado. As the new Sergeant-at-Arms for the 2011-2012 term, she looks forward to serving her club in an exemplary manner. Since joining Toastmasters, Shirley's confidence has grown by leaps and bounds, which has enabled her to better reach out to others. Shirley has owned and operated her own business as a child care director for the past thirty years, and is also a devoted 32-year member of the Holy Spirit Missionary Baptist Church. With leadership in her blood, Shirley has served as president of her church choir, usher board, youth board, youth director and member of the Pastors Aid Committee; she also has a fondness for fundraising and special events. Upon receiving a music scholarship to attend Langston University, Shirley earned her Bachelor of Science Degree in Elementary Education and Special Education from Metropolitan State College in Denver, Colorado. She is the seventh of fifteen children born to Ben and Pearl Washington in Swan Lake, Mississippi. She and her husband of thirty-six years, Jasper, are the proud parents of four biological children and one adopted child: Shana, Jasper III, Shanel, Justin and Richard. Married to a very loving man, they enjoy their eight beautiful grandchildren. Shirley enjoys spending time in home, church and Toastmaster activities; cooking, sports, traveling, singing, listening to music and laughing and having fun with her friends and family. She is a member of the Order of the Eastern Star, and is a local Mary Kay consultant.

Alice Austin: Alice joined the Absolutely Articulate Toastmasters Club #1272692, Aurora, Colorado, in 2009. She is widow to the late Toastmaster Joseph F. Austin. Alice is a retired secretary for Cherry Creek School District, and a former research assistant and volunteer for the Salvation Army. Active in church and community activities, Alice and her late husband served many years as devoted missionaries and traveled throughout Eastern Europe. In addition, she has unselfishly served as a board member representing the YWCA and a host of other local nonprofit organizations. She and Joe parented six biological children - Stan, Steve, Kathy, Joyce, Robert and Nancy - as well as about ten foster children. Her hobbies include writing, reading, antique browsing and spending time with family and friends.

Neisha Balleck: Neisha Balleck joined the Simply Speaking Toastmasters Club #667476 of Aurora, Colorado two years ago. She has served in two officer roles including Secretary and VP of Education. She has two associate degrees and currently works as a Registered Nurse on a cardiac and stroke observation floor. She enjoys caring for others and has a heart to help women and children harmed by violence and abuse. She currently is working with an organization called Hand of God Ministries that spiritually/financially adopts children in Ethiopia who have had one or both parents die from AIDS, and they are getting ready to start a new program to help mothers and children who are struggling to survive. Neisha is able to accomplish all of this because of the wonderful support she receives from her husband, Levi, and her two children, Ryan and Zuri.

Carolyn Betts: Carolyn Betts, who holds a Master of Arts in Psychology from Regis University (2009), is a professional speaker and former member of FACCMasters #5086, Toastmasters Club #5086, in Colorado Springs, Colorado. She has been a part of Toastmasters for more than 30 years, serving as Area Governor, and in most executive positions, winning numerous awards. After publishing her first work, Toastmasters became an essential factor in launching a twenty-five-plus year career as an orator. Carolyn's passionate love for life is expressed in her work as a sole proprietor, where she speaks, writes, emcees, and honors life as an Academic Certified Life Transitions Coach. A Scholarship recipient from the Colorado State Bar Association, she completed training as a Mediator. Her latest book, *A Special Kind of Normal, A Mother's Journey through Autism to Destiny*, 2010, has redefined her life's mission. As a tribute to others, she named her business Carolyn Betts You Can! (CBYC) Publications. She is connected to the American Business Women's Association (ABWA), via Colorado Springs Women's Express Network (CSWEN), the National Autism Society, and Peak Parenting. She is happily unmarried with adult children.

David Bounds: As a dual member of both the Absolutely Articulate Toastmasters Club #1272692 and Simply Speaking Toastmasters Club #677476, David currently serves as the Creative Director for the Simply Speaking Toastmasters Club where he has maintained his membership for five years. Some of David's unique art collection was recently on display at the Absolutely Articulate Toastmasters Club "Toastmaster of the Year" black tie formal event and was seen by hundreds of guests. Toastmaster David Bounds is a two-time second place winner of the District's Humorous Speech Contest, and is known far and wide for his talented ability to make others laugh and learn. Raised in Texas, he worked as an Art Director in Dallas and is recognized as a gifted and talented artist and teacher. Working as an art instructor for a local Christian school, David enjoys working with youngsters while showing them creative ways to express themselves. He is a graduate of the University of Texas in Austin with a major in art and advertising and is known for notoriously adding his magical touch to every project that he is assigned. He and wife Joanne are the proud parents of two brilliant college students. David's hobbies include spending time with family and friends, tennis, fishing and, of course, making people laugh.

Marcy Brack: Marcy Brack currently serves as President of the Simply Speaking Toastmasters Club #677476 located in Aurora, Colorado. Coming from a family line of Toastmasters including her dad and twin sister, Marcy is very close to earning her Advanced Communication-Bronze and Advanced Leadership-Bronze award. Marcy has worked as a registered nurse for over 30 years and is passionate about delivering quality health care. She currently works as the manager of a clinic, and thoroughly enjoys passing on the spirit of passion while mentoring her staff. The mother of two fabulous children ages 25 and 19, Marcy's hobbies include oil painting, writing and working out as a conscientious fitness person. Marcy is a native of Maryland, and has lived in beautiful Colorado for 30 years. Her goal has always been to write a whimsical book about lessons learned as a result of her full and interesting life.

Emma Bretz: Emma Bretz is a thirteen-year-old who just graduated from a local junior high; she is the daughter of Joan Janis, president of the Cherry Creek Toastmasters. Emma is an aspiring artist who loves to read, write, and draw. In mid July, she will turn 14, and hopes to beat her mother out for the White Ribbon in the Toastmasters Club

Table Topics club competition at least once more before then; she's already got one under her belt.

Lee E. Brown, Jr.: Lee Brown is a friend of the Absolutely Articulate Toastmasters Club located in Aurora, Colorado. He is a native of Kansas City, Missouri and has enjoyed living in the Rocky Mountain Colorado area for over 30 years. As a professional saxophonist and educator, Lee is the husband of an Absolutely Articulate Toastmaster, and serves as one of the city's talented musicians. Following in his father's musical footsteps, Lee thoroughly enjoys music and teaches and tutors others in this field. His dad (Lee, Sr.) was honored in Kansas City along with other elder statesmen for performing and promoting the Kansas City style of jazz and blues. Among the list of honorees were luminaries such as William "Count Basie", Charlie Parker, et al. As a seasoned public school educator and accomplished musician, Lee, Jr. has performed (and recorded) with some of the finest gospel and jazz musicians throughout the rocky mountain region. Lee received his education from Metro State College and Lesley College. He is married to his Kansas City, high school sweetheart and they fellowship at True Light Baptist Church in Denver, Colorado. Lee served as a distinguished instructor with the Denver's "Jazz Garden Project" that taught aspiring teen musicians jazz, sponsored by AALI and 104.3 FM cool jazz radio. Based on his exceptional work to serve as an effective catalyst to instruct and motivate students, Lee was named "Middle School Educator of the Year" by The EduCtr in 2011. When he is not teaching or performing, Lee Brown spends his spare time having fun with his family and friends, playing his favorite instrument and tutoring students in music.

Leroy Brown: Leroy Brown is a member of Absolutely Articulate Toastmasters Club #1272692 located in Aurora, Colorado. A God-fearing man and trustee at his home church, he is a retired Denver Public Schools educator.

Leroy is a graduate with a Bachelor of Arts in Education from Central Missouri State University and a master's degree in Special Education from the University of Northern Colorado-Greeley. A native of St. Louis, Missouri, he has been happily married for 31 years and is the father of a wonderful, musically talented son. Leroy is a member of the Mile High Chapter Theater Company and enjoys sports, singing (in 3 groups), film critic, helping others including active with his church food bank ministry and praising God.

Gina Curley: Gina Curley is a member of Night Speakers Toastmasters Club #810454 located in Longmont, Colorado. She received her Distinguished Toastmaster Award in 2010. Gina has worked in the IT industry for twenty years and is currently employed at Oracle Corporation as a Senior Technical Support Engineer. In addition to her work and Toastmasters, Gina is a volunteer Speaking Ambassador for the American Red Cross. In 2007, Gina graduated from the University of Phoenix with a degree in Business Administration. She has been married to her best friend, Hugh Curley, for 11 years. Gina enjoys reading and spending time with Hugh in their beautiful quiet home located in a rural area near the foothills of the Rocky Mountains.

Sherise Frank: Sherise Frank is a member of the Absolutely Articulate Toastmasters Club #1272692 located in Aurora, Colorado. Sherise works as a Quality Assurance Evaluator for Specialized Loan Servicing. She is a graduate of Rangeview High School, and attended Pickens Technical College in 2005 where she received her certificate and professional Colorado license as an esthetician. In 2010, she competed in the Mrs. Colorado Pageant in 2010 with plans to compete again until she accomplishes her goal of being crowned Mrs. Colorado. Sherise has been married to her best friend for thirteen years, and they are the parents of three beautiful children. Sherise enjoys spending time with her family, vacationing and just sitting in a quiet room doing absolutely nothing!

Renee Franklin: Renee Franklin is a charter member of the Absolutely Articulate Toastmasters Club #1272692 located in Aurora, Colorado where she has served in the club officer capacity of VP-Education and Treasurer. As a fourth-generation Colorado native, she and her two brothers were privileged to be raised by their loving and devoted mother. Renee is the proud mother of one daughter, Maria, and two grandchildren, Marquis and Fiona, who are the loves of her life. She is also the primary caregiver for her beloved mother. Renee was educated in the Denver Public School system and attended Emily Griffin Opportunity School, Denver University and New Beginning Cathedral School of Ministry. She is the owner of Expert Nursing and Companion Service/Absolutely Home Health Care where she has proudly served seniors and people with disabilities for the past twenty-six years. Having served as an evangelist for the past sixteen years, Renee was recently ordained as an Elder at the House of Joy Miracle Deliverance Church. She has also worked in a service capacity for more than twenty-five years in the prison and nursing home ministries. Renee is the recipient of a number of community and business awards based on her exceptional generosity, outreach and exemplary service to help others in need.

Betty A. Funderburke: Betty is a dual member of the Absolutely Articulate Toastmasters Club #1272692 and Aurorators Toastmasters Club #2136, both located in Aurora, Colorado. As co-founder of the Absolutely Articulate Club, Betty also served as Past District Secretary for District 26 in the 2009-2010 term. Having served in many leadership roles in toastmaster clubs, Betty was named "Toastmaster of the Year" in 2010 for her unselfish, exceptional work to mentor and help all members to learn and excel. In 2010, Betty earned her Distinguished Toastmaster Award (DTM), the highest honor that can be earned by a member of Toastmasters International. She currently works as a Host Home Provider and is responsible for two physically and mentally challenged young adults. In addition, she is co-founder of the Sisters Enterprise Annual Back Home Gospel Shout Out program. Betty was nominated for the Juanita Gray Community Service Award, and is the recipient of the Denver Urban Spectrum *"African Americans Who Make a Difference"* award. She is also the recipient of the 2011 Zeta Phi Beta Sorority Community Service Award and 2011 Multicultural Mother's Day Award sponsored by the Red Line Museum in Denver. She is a long-time member of Denver's Free Indeed Deliverance Ministry, Ambassadors for Christ and currently serves as a distinguished colleague of the African American Leadership Institute class of 2011. While serving as a volunteer with the American Red Cross organization, Betty thoroughly enjoys her outreach work to help the poor and disadvantaged. A native of Kansas City, Missouri, Betty fervently believes that charity begins at home. Mrs. Funderburke is married, and is the mother of two adult sons and four grandchildren. Betty enjoys spending time with her family, friends and devoting time to church activities as well as writing, singing and performing with the Mile High Chapter Theater Company. This aspiring artist who refuses to stop learning desires to become an inspirational speaker. As always, she relies on God for guidance and leadership.

Virginia Glist: Mrs. Glist first joined Toastmasters International in April, 2005, and is currently a member of the Toast-A-Matics Toastmasters Club #1120162. Born on October 9, 1920, in White Lake, South Dakota, Virginia is a retired high school teacher of English, drama and speech, and earned her Bachelors and Masters Degree from Indiana University where she majored in literature. This academic scholar is the author of 2 books –*Lend an Ear* (1983) and *Sugar Plum* (1994). She is the mother of one son (deceased), and has lived in the beautiful, rocky mountain Colorado area for the past thirty-five years. As an honorable World War II veteran of the U.S. Army, she proudly served her country as a medical laboratory technician. This ninety-year-old accomplished Toastmaster currently holds an Advanced Communicator Gold Award in the Toastmasters organization. When she is not working on another award winning speech, this inspiring Toastmaster enjoys reading and attending her Toast-a-Matics Toastmasters Club that meets every Thursday at 12:00 noon at the Anschutz Medical Campus. Voted Best Speaker at her Toast-a-Matics Club in the International Speech & Table Topics Contest, Toastmaster, Virginia recently competed in the Area International competition held in April 2011 in Aurora.

Elizabeth Hall: Information not available.

Gail Hamilton: Gail was born visually impaired in 1953 to upper-middle class parents in Indianapolis, Indiana. She is a devoted member of ToastAbility Toastmasters Club #863184 located in Denver, Colorado. As a professional, polished speaker, she has competed in past Toastmaster speech competitions and enjoyed numerous honors and accolades for her outstanding speaking and leadership ability. Through her heartwarming, provocative stories, this multi-talented professional demonstrates how obstacles, challenges, and daily struggles can be transformed into options and celebrations. After hearing Gail's incredible life story, audiences leave with a desire to persevere, to bring more passion into their life, to create endless possibilities and a heightened desire to rise above obstacles with new vision. Gail has enjoyed teaching beginning piano, voice, and autoharp to kids and adults in the Denver community for twenty-nine years. Her specialty lies in teaching students to play by ear or by sheet music, popular or classical. As a talented vocalist, pianist and auto harpist, this amazing woman of many talents has a powerful voice, artistic sensitivity, and a broad versatility of styles which spans the musical spectrum from folk and pop to light opera and classical. Gail earned her Bachelor of Arts degree from William Woods University in Fulton, Missouri, and a Master of Music degree with emphasis in vocal performance from Pittsburg State University in Pittsburg, Kansas. After pursuing doctoral studies in voice at the University of Boulder, she changed fields and acquired a Master of Arts degree in psychology and counseling from the Naropa Institute in Boulder. Gail enjoys giving motivational presentations combining acting, art and music to tell her story, and is currently composing a CD and completing a nonfiction, inspirational book of courage and perseverance, *Wings to Fly, A Story of* .... Born with many gifts, this amazing, powerful woman draws on her inner resources of light, joy, unity, love, power, promise and peace to manifest her outer vision of bringing hope and inspiration to others to empower others to spread their wings and fly. With ease, grace and joy, Gail is a superb speaker and performer for all occasions - banquets, church solos, club or organization engagements, conventions, private parties, school assemblies or weddings.

Pamela Hertzog: Pamela Hertzog is a dual member of two Toastmasters clubs: Ranch Raconteurs #873616 of Highland Ranch, Colorado, and Spirited Speakers #1440289 of Centennial, Colorado. When Pam was a member of the Simply Speaking #677476 Toastmaster Club, she served as club president during the 2007-2008 term. Pam is an accomplished writer, speaker and coach. Having earned her Toastmasters Advanced Communication Gold award and Advanced Leadership Bronze award, she is known throughout the district as a "go-to" person for humor and creativity. Pam has three adult sons and is proud of completing a Masters degree in Communication in 2004, but her real "baby" is her one-woman show, The G.A.L. Show (for Gracefully Aging Ladies). It is a collection of song parodies and humorous monologues around the topic of aging. Because there is a lot to laugh about, Pam wants to provide healing and hope through humor. You can schedule a "salon performance" of the show with your friends by contacting her at: pamela_hertzog@yahoo.com.

Donna Hilton: Donna Hilton served as the 2010-2011 President of Aurorators Club #2136 located in Aurora,

Colorado and is also a member of the Absolutely Articulate #1272692 Toastmasters Club, also located in Aurora, Colorado. Donna helped to spearhead the literary book project that resulted in *Lift As You Climb*. Donna currently serves as a Grants Manager for Food Bank of the Rockies, and is a board member for the Emergency Food and Shelter Board and Street Smart Youth Mentoring Group. As a proud member of the Delta Sigma Theta Sorority, she was recognized as the 2009 Winner of the National Leadership Award (National Business Advisory Council). This high achiever earned her Bachelor of Arts degree in 1994 from the University of Colorado-Boulder. Donna is single (although *thinking* about adding a cat to her family of one), an avid sports fanatic, movie buff and enjoys dabbling in politics as an outside supporter of the best candidates on the city, state and national slate.

Tom G. Hobbs: Tom Hobbs is a member of member of Gates to Excellence Toastmasters #3413 located in Denver, Colorado where he is recognized as a Distinguished Toastmaster (DTM). Tom is a self-employed entrepreneurial nut, professional speaker, dance host and instructor. As a member of Gates to Excellence Toastmasters, Denver Colorado he has been recognized as a Distinguished Toastmaster (DTM). Completing his term as Denver Division Governor, Tom was recently selected as the new District Lieutenant Governor of Marketing for District 26. Tom's joy of dance has taken him on many cruise ships as a Dance Host. Dancing on 5 different continents and visiting nearly 100 countries, he has met some of the most amazing people in the world. Their stories and experiences continue to shape Tom's life. As a young country boy, he never imagined visiting Antarctica,

Easter Island, Europe, or Hawaii. Tom takes these experiences and speaks to youth of all ages. He also utilizes the many skills gained while serving as a District Leader in Toastmasters International. While infusing all of this with his high power enthusiasm and encouraging all to succeed, he is known as the *Man in the Hat* - a cool thing to be known for.

Joan Janis: Joan is a member of Cherry Creek Toastmasters #2977 in Denver, Colorado. She has served as Sergeant-At-Arms and two terms as club President. Joan joined Toastmasters in June, 2008, and has since earned her Advanced Communicator Bronze as well as her Competent Leader awards. As a winning contestant in Toastmasters International speech contests, Joan has won first place in her club for three years in a row, as well as competed at area, division, and district level contests. She is the 2011 Champion of Public Speaking for the Denver Division. Joan is a mentor to several members of her club, as well as a friend to many Toastmasters clubs in metropolitan Denver. Joan Janis is the owner of BretzTEC Computer and Network Specialists, a tech support company that has been serving small businesses in Denver for 10 years. She and her husband of 31 years, Jeff Bretz, have two children, Emma and Joey. Joan is a participating member of SUBUD USA, a teacher of Rudra meditation, and the Education Coordinator for the Greater Denver Group chapter of Business Network International (BNI).

Iffie Jennings: Iffie Jennings is a member of the Aurorators Toastmasters #2136 Club located in Aurora, Colorado, where she serves as VP-Public Relations. Currently working at Kaiser Permanente as a Wellness

Consultant, Iffie is a member of the Delta Sigma Theta Sorority, Inc. She earned her Bachelor of Science degree from the Colorado State University with a major in Health and Exercise and her Master of Business Administration degree from Regis University in 2008. Married to the love of her life, Rayshun Jennings, they enjoy one son, Rayshun Jennings, Jr. Iffie's favorite pastime is exercising and spending time with family and friends.

Kumu Keindaswamy: Kumu is a dual member of the Absolutely Articulate #1272692 and Simply Speaking #677476 Toastmaster Clubs both located in Aurora, Colorado. She is past Sergeant at Arms for the SS Club and will serve as the club's VP Public Relations in the upcoming year. Kumu is from Siruvani, India, and recently earned her MBA in health management from the University of Colorado. She has lived in Colorado for the past five years, and is the oldest in her family of two. As a professional who is passionate about health care matters, she currently works in the health care industry. In her spare time, Kumu enjoys gardening, karaoke and dancing. The "Lift As You Climb" book is Kumu's first book project.

Pattie Koop: Pattie Koop, Advanced Communication-Silver and Competent Leadership certification, has been a proud member of the Pioneer #2932 Toastmasters Club located in Lakewood, Colorado for the past 6 years. She has held every club officer position except for treasurer. Although she has held the honorable leadership position of area governor, she is currently enjoying her role as a P.O.T. (Plain Old Toastmaster). While working as a self-employed entrepreneur, Pattie is beginning to consider retirement in order to spend more time getting acquainted with newly discovered and geographically scattered birth family. She has a Bachelor of Science degree in Behavioral Psychology, earned in 1990 from Charter Oak College in Connecticut. Pattie is married, has two grown children, four grand-children, and one great-grandchild. Her hobbies include genealogy, travel, spending quality time with the household pets, reading, creative writing, social networking and, of course, Toastmasters International.

Elaine Love: Elaine Love is a member of the Meridian Mid Day Toast #7326 (Englewood, CO), Spirited Speakers #1440289 (Centennial, CO) and Speak Up #6015 (Colorado Springs, CO) clubs. She is a former Metro Area Governor, current Metro Division Governor for Toastmasters International District 26. She amazingly earned her Distinguished Toastmaster Award in 30 months and will receive the Triple Crown award for 2011 (most individual educational awards received in 2011 for District 26.) Elaine placed second on the fourth level of a six level contest for World Champion of Public Speaking in her fifth month in Toastmasters. Elaine has owned Candy Mountain Culinary Creations and Mountain Castles Property Management; she currently owns and operates L.E. Love, Inc. and Results for Life LLC. Elaine enjoys her profession of keynote speaking, training, workshops and business coaching with the business name of "Tiger in High Heels." She is program chairman for Castle Pines Rotary, serves on the vestry of Good Shepherd Episcopal Church and is an Ambassador for Castle Pines Chamber of Commerce and Main Street Chamber. Elaine served as Ambassador for Steamboat Springs, Colorado Chamber of Commerce, Strings in the Mountains Guild and as Docent for the Steamboat Arts Council for over a decade. Her degrees include a Bachelor of Science in Education with a double major and double minor from Kansas State College of Pittsburg; she graduated in 3 years with a Superior Student designation. Elaine also earned a Masters Degree of Applied Communication and Advanced Studies in Alternative Dispute Resolution from the University of Denver. Her master's thesis, "Marketing Reservations for Property Management on the Internet," was published in 1997 with 3 years of her company history included. Elaine has a plethora of published articles and videos; she achieved beyond Expert Author status to the Platinum author ranking. She also earned the designations of Real Estate Broker, M3 Master Consultant and Toastmaster of the Year. Elaine is the proud mother of Doug Love and Dan Love as well as proud grandmother to Gus, Gordon, Kaden and Kyler. This extraordinary, polished and caring professional loves public speaking, training, coaching, mentoring, music, dancing, telemark skiing, hiking and being an exerciseaholic.

Stephanie Lynn: Stephanie Lynn first started her toastmasters career with the Cherry Creek Toastmasters Club #2977 located in Denver, Colorado and later joined the Absolutely Articulate #1272692 Toastmasters Club located in Aurora, Colorado. After earning her Competent Communication first award after five months in the Toastmasters organization, Stephanie stood out as a polished, articulate and dynamic public speaker. In 2010, she earned the Best Speaker Award at the Absolutely Articulate International Club contest and went on to compete at the Area Contest level. As a highly sought-after speaker from southwest Louisiana who is proud of her Cajun heritage, Stephanie touches her audience with a sweet Southern accent and a transparency that is refreshing in today's image-oriented society. While delivering her keynotes and life coaching with side-splitting humor, enthusiasm and wisdom, this author, speaker, life coach, personal trainer and articulate toastmaster has spoken to hundreds on refusing to settle for less than they deserve in every area of their life. Stephanie is a member of the National Life Coaching Association and Core Energy Leadership Institution. She is author of *Embracing Life's Roses Through the Thorns*, (September 2011) and co-author with Stephen Covey of *Success Simplified* (August 2011). Because Stephanie has learned to live life on purpose, not "on accident," her experiences and genuine compassion for others has seasoned her for coaching. Stephanie teaches her students how to position every circumstance, even the tragic ones, to form a purposeful landscape in their lives. By maneuvering them into helping themselves, she helps to identify their own deep rooted beliefs, attitudes, and inhibitions that prevent them from their full potential. Stephanie is an expert in empowering people to move beyond loss or disappointment and begin to walk courageously into the future. As the founder of a new bullying program known as CHANGE, her transformational weekend with adolescents focuses on the pressures and choices that will shape their futures. Stephanie is a graduate of the University of Lafayette and holds a Bachelor of Science degree in business administration: marketing; she also is a graduate of the New England Life Coaching School. This single mother of two beautiful children, Lacey, 25, and Ross, 22, enjoys playing tennis and participating in Cross Fit Fitness classes. For more information on how to bring Stephanie to your city or youth group, you may go to her website at stephanielynnspeaking.com.

Jose "George" Maestas: George Maestas is currently a dual member of the Simply Speaking Toastmasters Club #67747 and the Absolutely Articulate Toastmasters Club #1272692 located in Aurora, Colorado; he is also a former member of Orbiting Toasters Club #6656. George Maestas grew up in northern New Mexico and has two talented and gifted children (Alicen and Vidal) whom he loves with all his heart. As an entrepreneur and business owner of Green H2o Well LLC, George inspires and helps people discover better health and vitality. In addition, he has been instrumental in helping people with hard water concerns that can damage equipment. Based on his background that includes 25 years experience as a systems engineer for a major corporation, he is recognized as a subject matter expert on water and how it relates to personal health. In his spare time, George enjoys various forms of exercise such as yoga, pilates, tai chi, hiking, bicycling, walking and meditation. For more information about Green H2o, go to www.greenh2owell.com.

Katey McEniry: Katey is a 14-year-old sophomore at a local high school, and has served as a volunteer for the Absolutely Articulate Toastmasters Club for two years. A triplet, Katey was blessed with two endearing fraternal brothers as well as a big brother who is 18 years old. A native of Georgia, Katey has enjoyed beautiful Colorado since she relocated to this region with her family at age 4. As a former victim of bullying, Katey believes that she can make a positive difference in the world by being a good and kind role model and making sure that bullies don't intimidate others. Katey's favorite subject in school is English, and her hobbies include swimming, dancing, singing, reading, writing and doing volunteer work for one of the local toastmasters clubs. Following in her mother's footsteps (a school teacher), Katey would like to be a physical education coach when she grows up.

Troi Mullins: Troi Mullins is a member of Absolutely Articulate Club #1272692 of Aurora, Colorado. She currently works for Jackson Ice Cream, a subsidiary of Kroger, where she holds the position of Training Coordinator. Troi is a member of Jack & Jill of America, Denver Chapter, and the Order of the Eastern Stars. She has a Masters in HR Management and is currently pursuing a second graduate degree in Management and Leadership with Webster University. She is married with three beautiful children.

Edwin Pens: Ed Pens is an enthusiastic, grateful and dual member of Gates to Excellence Toastmasters #3413 located in Denver, Colorado, and Simply Speaking Toastmasters #677476 located in Aurora, Colorado. He is the founder of *IntroduceYourself!.org*; some of his co–creators can be viewed at IntroduceYourselfNow on YouTube. As a self-employed mason and carpenter, this entrepreneur specializes in historically sensitive repairs and remodels on Victorian and other Classic Style homes from Curtis Park to Arapahoe Acres in the metropolitan Denver area. Ed typically works directly with the homeowner, and is glad to consult with and advise the owner on the areas of his expertise. With over twelve years focused on the structures built between 1880 and 1955, he has thirty-five years' experience in general masonry and framing. He is the father of one daughter and is the proud grandfather of two.

Cassandra Perkins: Cassie Perkins is the 14-year-old daughter of Toastmaster Joni Perkins, member of Absolutely Articulate Toastmaster Club #1272692 located in Aurora, Colorado. Cassandra learned about Toastmasters as a result of receiving a random act of kindness award for making a difference in her community. Realizing how difficult it can sometimes be to speak in front of others, Cassandra visits the Absolutely Articulate Club with her mother, Joni Perkins in order to learn how to be more versatile and competent as a public speaker. Nine years ago, this 5-year-old, brown-eyed tomboy hit the small theatrical stage in Parker, Colorado where she performed in 7 productions. By the age of 10, Cassandra had blossomed into a fine young actor with several IMDB film credits to her name as well as a Heartland Regional Emmy nomination. Cassandra is an active member of the Asgard Stunt team where she performs film-related fight choreography, weapons technique (knife, sword and run) and high/low fall techniques. She is also an active member of the "Youth 4 Parker" – a young city council committee that coordinates community outreach. At age 14, Cassandra, who has her own internet talk show that speaks out to teens and other individuals on topics of interest that the public needs to hear about, has the ultimate goal to positively impact the lives of the people around her while boldly standing up and speaking out in her community.

Joni Perkins: Joni is a member of the Absolutely Articulate Toastmasters Club #1272692 located in Aurora, Colorado. Joni was attracted to Toastmasters due to her

14-year-old daughter, Cassandra. As a mentor and responsible mother, Joni realized that she needed the speaking tools to speak in front of the media and other public figures. A graduate of Arapahoe Community College, Joni enjoys photography and managing her daughter's acting career. Joni is married to her husband of sixteen years, Burgess, and together they have two children, Cassandra and Alyssa. When they are not filming or volunteering in their community of Parker, Colorado, they enjoy free time at their cabin, fishing, boating and taking in the sunny weather of beautiful, colorful Colorado. Joni is a native of Waterloo, Iowa, and she just completed her first book project.

Denette Polk: Denette Polk has been a member of the Aurorators Toastmasters Club #2136 located in Aurora, Colorado since July, 2009. Since this time, she served in the club officer position of Club Secretary and continues to be an active member. She is currently employed with the United States Treasury as an ACS Representative in Denver, Colorado. Denette is also a member of the Christ for Life Drama Ministry, where she has had the opportunity to serve in leading roles; this organization regularly provides theatrical plays throughout the community, in which she has held lead roles. Trained in basic disaster response skills, such as disaster preparedness, first aid, fire suppression, medical operations, and light search and rescue operations, Denette is also a member of CERT (Community Emergency Response Team). Denette received her Associate in Applied Science with a major in accounting in 2005, and is currently enrolled at the University of Phoenix. Denette is single and is the mother of two children and one granddaughter. She enjoys spending time with her family and friends as well as members of her toastmasters club. *Lift As You Climb* is Denette's first book project.

Elinora L. Reynolds: Elinora is a member of Absolutely Articulate Toastmasters Club #1272692 located in Aurora, Colorado, and she is co-founder and immediate past president of the Absolutely Articulate Club where she serves as friend and mentor to many. She was named "Governor of the Year" in 2009 after serving as the Area Governor in the M-1 Aurora area and named "Toastmaster of the Year" in 2004 by her first home club. Elinora later earned her Distinguished Toastmaster (DTM) award in 2009, the highest honor that can be earned by a member of the Toastmasters International organization. She currently works as an event planner and grant writer for nonprofit organizations in the metro Denver/Aurora area. While working at the Colorado Department of Transportation, her award-winning traffic safety programs received national recognition. Elinora is past president of the National Association of Business & Professional Women and is a recipient of the Who's Who of Women and Who's Who of Professional Management awards. During her college years, she was inducted into the Phi Theta Kappa Honor Society. Elinora has served on a plethora of local nonprofit boards as a devoted volunteer committed to helping the poor and disadvantaged, and she thoroughly enjoys serving as a volunteer with the American Red Cross organization. With state and federal government work experience, this foot soldier was honored to formerly serve in Denver's precinct #1108 as a committeewoman and devoted public servant. She is co-founder of the city's Annual Back Home Gospel Shout Out event that gives random acts of kindness awards to local honorees. Elinora earned her Bachelor of Science Degree from the University of Missouri and Masters Degree from Central Michigan University where she majored in Business Administration; she later earned post-graduate credit at the University of Denver. She is a member of True Light Baptist Church, Ambassadors for Christ and African American Leadership Institute. Her published works include *Mental Health: Counseling Services from a Black Perspective, a Selected Annotated Bibliography* (1987), as well as a number of published poetry submissions. Elinora is the youngest in her large family of nine, and is wife to her high school sweetheart, Lee. She credits God, her family-rearing in Kansas City, Missouri, and exceptional training through the Toastmasters organization for her ability to effectively stand up and speak out. Her hobbies include poetry, chess, engaging in church and family activities, creative writing and thinking and reaching out to help others. Elinora proudly carries her late mother's name, who taught her to always Lift As You Climb.

J. Christine Richards: J. Christine Richards is a member of Castle Rock Toastmasters Club #3680. In her four-year membership, she has been the VP of Education for two years and President for the past year. She loves mentoring new members and is looking forward to being a mentor to the board of officers in the coming year. She has competed at both club and Area levels in the International Speech Contest, the Evaluation Contest, and the Table Topics Contest. Known to her friends as Chris, she is an author of Christian suspense, devotionals, and Bible studies. She was a journalist for the Sterling Journal Advocate for three years. One of her stories was published in an anthology about Whitby Abbey in England, titled *Whitby Abbey - Pure Inspiration*. She recently started Passing the Quill, LLC with the goal of helping young writers accomplish their dreams of becoming authors. Another way she helps youth is as a volunteer judge for home school speech competitions. She keeps her hands busy with various types of needlework for friends, family, the homeless and those in need. Mrs. Richards has been married for forty-three years, has three daughters, five grandsons, and one granddaughter, all living close enough where she can get her "grandma fix" whenever she desires. Her hobbies are writing, photography, hiking, and needlework. She is the president of the Mile High Scribes Chapter (South Denver) of the American Christian Fiction Writers and on the leadership board of Words for the Journey Christian Writers Guild. She is on the volunteer team for the Douglas County Libraries Writers Conference and the Colorado Christian Writers Conference.

James P. Seballes: James Seballes first joined toastmasters in 2008 and is a charter member of the Defenders of Speech #897557 Toastmasters Club which originated on Buckley AFB, Colorado. There he served as a member of the council, holding the position of treasurer. James is currently in the Air Force, having served faithfully for seventeen years. He is originally from the great state of Texas; born in Fort Worth, Texas, he was raised in the capital city of Austin. His service currently has taken him and his family to the outback of Australia. However, he has served overseas in the country of Japan, as well as stateside in Arizona and Colorado. James is married to his best friend of nearly twenty-four years, and this fall they will celebrate their 16th wedding anniversary. Together they have been blessed with three beautiful boys, Alek, 13; James, Jr., 4; and Ari, 1. James enjoys watching sports, being outdoors and spending time with his beautiful family.

Margaret Seyer: Margaret Seyer joined the Simply Speaking #677476 Toastmasters Club in 2005; she has served as a leader in her favorite club in the club officer capacity of Sergeant at Arms and Treasurer. She has also been active in past international club contests. A native of Queens, New York, Margaret has lived in Colorado for 15 years. She has worked in retail customer service for Target for the past three years. Among her accomplishments, Margaret earned her Toastmasters Competent Communication award last year and is currently working toward completion of her Competent Leadership award. With a great appreciation for children, she completed her childcare internship from Molloy College in Long Island, New York. Margaret enjoys her single life and in her spare time, she enjoys bicycle riding, roller skating, movies, travel and spending time with friends and family. As an auntie six times over, she loves to hang out with her beloved nieces and nephews - Abby, Hannah, Gi Gi, Matthew, Alex and Joshua. Her best friend and companion, Larry, is a 4-year-old Chihuahua who loves to eat, exercise and play games. Margaret is an active member of Rolling Hills Community Church.

Roy Shankle: Roy Shankle is an advanced member of the Absolutely Articulate #1272692 Toastmasters Club, located in Aurora, Colorado. Roy works in sales, and is also a part-time student at Westwood College where he is pursuing a major in IT Security Systems & Networking. The proud father of two ten-year-old sons, he is married to his best friend, Ayana. Roy is a native of Kansas City, Missouri, and in his spare time, enjoys writing, public speaking and, of course, spending time with his family and friends. He is a devoted member of Free Indeed Deliverance Ministry.

Ron Shuster: Ron Shuster is a member of WryToast Toastmasters #8358 located in Greenwood Village, Colorado. He is a retired public school teacher. Ron is a member of the School Board at DCS Montessori Charter School. Additionally, he volunteers at each of his grandson's schools and operates a small landscape business. Ron is a co-author of *Celebrating 365 Days of Gratitude*. He graduated from the University of Colorado and has a Master's Degree in Communication from the University of Northern Colorado. Ron has been married for over forty years and has two grandsons, Tanner and Conner. Since retiring, Ron has enjoyed traveling. He has been to Belize twice, taken a cruise in the Caribbean, seen the Sand Hill Crane migration in Nebraska, and gone to Mexico for a week of language instruction while his wife was at a Yoga retreat. Two years ago, Ron took his grandson, Tanner, on a cruise to Mexico and this year, it will be Conner's turn to sail the Caribbean with his grandfather. Ron enjoys playing tennis, reading, and spending time with his wife. Ron is working on his next book, *Retirement for Regular Guys – Real Men Tell the Truth about Real Retirement*.

Annette Sills-Brown: Annette Sills-Brown is a member of Absolutely Articulate #1272692 Club, located in Aurora, Colorado. As a child of God, she is a minister in the AME

Zion church and a member of many organizations. Annette is a caring, skilled, devoted teacher who goes the extra mile for her students as a Denver Public Schools educator of seventeen years. This high achiever graduated from the University of Phoenix with a dual degree in Business Management and Business Administration. She also holds a master's degree in Education -Curriculum from the University of Phoenix, and is certified as a principal in the State of Colorado. She has won several awards including the 2010 Excellence in Education Award (Colorado Gospel Music Awards), Parents of Excellence Award Colorado 2008, and Salute to Excellence in Education "Harriett Tubman" Award, 2011. A native of St. Louis, Missouri, Annette is the mother of one musically talented son. She performs with the Mile High Chapter Theater Company, and also enjoys singing, reading, cooking, fighting for civil rights and being a helpmate and best friend to her husband of thirty-one years.

Pamela Y. Simmons: Pamela Simmons is a member of Absolutely Articulate Toastmasters #1272692 located in Aurora, Colorado. Pam has lived in Denver, Colorado, for twenty-four years, and works for a public sector organization in Human Resources. Pam enjoys learning and being challenged, and seeks opportunities for professional growth and development. In her spare time, she enjoys spending time with her family, volunteering, participating in and attending sporting events, traveling, reading and going to the spa. Pam's highest priority and greatest achievement is raising her daughter, Sierra, who attends a local high school.

Sierra C. Simmons: Sierra Simmons lives in Denver, Colorado, and is a junior at a local high school in Aurora, Colorado. Sierra is the daughter of Pamela Simmons, member of the Absolutely Articulate Toastmasters club, and enjoys visiting the toastmasters club while learning how the professionals do it. She enjoys spending time with her family (including her cat, Smooches), volunteering in the nursery at her church and staying active in school activities. A talented artist and photographer, Sierra plans to pursue a career in the fashion industry.

Abigail Smucker: Abigail is a member of Simply Speaking #677476 Toastmasters in Aurora, Colorado, and served as Vice-President of Public Relations for one year. She volunteered in several capacities for speech competitions in Toastmasters International, and enjoys the club's team-building and leadership development opportunities. Abigail is a solo bankruptcy law practitioner in the greater Denver area.

Alan Swartz: Alan Swartz is a member of Simply Speaking Toastmasters #677476 (Aurora, CO), Summit Toastmasters #7064 (Frisco, CO), Excelsior Toastmasters #3247 (Lakewood, CO) and Eagle Valley Toastmasters #146508 (Avon, CO). He served as Area Governor of the Year in 2007; Division Governor of the Year in 1987; Distinguished Toastmaster in 1989 and 2010; Foothills Division Governor, 2007-2008; Lieutenant Governor Education and Training, 2008-2009; and District 26 Governor, 2009-2010. Alan works for the Teller Park Conservation District in Woodland Park as Weed Management Coordinator. He is also a member of the Colorado Weed Management Association; President of the

Upper Arkansas Valley Cooperative Weed Management Area; past President of the Colorado Association of Extension 4-H Agents; Colorado County Agents Association; FarmHouse Fraternity at Purdue; and a retired lieutenant colonel in the U.S. Army. Alan graduated from Purdue University with a Bachelor of Science in Ag Science in 1965 and a Masters in Counseling from Ball State University in 1972. He is married to the fabulous and talented Connie Akins. He has two children, Roxanna Nicoll, who is a dentist, and George Dustin Swartz, who does singing telegrams, entertains, and writes for 303 magazines. Alan is a skier, a reader, a movie buff and cans great salsa while enjoying speaking and helping other Toastmasters.

Vanessa Thomas-Jones: Vanessa Thomas-Jones is a member of Absolutely Articulate Toastmasters Club #1272692 located in Aurora, Colorado, where she was recently elected as the new 2011-2012 club president. As an exceptional Toastmaster Competent Communicator, Vanessa successfully won first place in the 2011 International Table Topics Competition and second place in the International Speech Competition while representing the Absolutely Articulate Toastmasters Club. Vanessa is Manager of AQP Systems Support at United Airlines completing her twenty-fifth company anniversary in 2010. In addition, she is a Senior Tax Preparer at H & R Block (seasonally) and manages her personal business as a Licensed Colorado Realtor specializing in Foreclosure Intervention and Short Sales. Her academic credentials include an Executive Master of Business Administration from The Daniels College of Business, University of Denver and a Bachelor of Arts in Communication from the

University of Denver. Additionally, Vanessa considers herself a Lifelong Learner. Vanessa is married to Warren Jones, with four children - Patrick, Darton, Crystal Connally and Angel Holt – and the proud grandmother of two. Her dream is to open a superior childcare center dedicated to enhancing all children's' ability to learn and to grow to be extraordinary, spiritual human beings. A Denver native, Vanessa is a proud member of Alpha Kappa Alpha Sorority and attends Emmanuel Christian Center. Her favorite things include playing with her grandchildren, international travel, volunteering, learning new technologies and Nestlé's Quik chocolate milk.

Mike Thompson: Mike Thompson is a member of Absolutely Articulate Toastmasters Club #1272692 located in Aurora, Colorado. He was selected as the "Best Speaker" in the 2011 Toastmasters International Absolutely Articulate Speech and finished in top two in the Table Topics Contest. Mike currently serves as VP-Public Relations for the Absolutely Articulate Toastmasters Club. As the CEO/Founder of The Father's Show Resource Program that was launched in November 2004, he is also well known in the Denver/Aurora area for his work as a motivational speaker, mentor, model, singer and activist. This single father of four has been featured in numerous local publications regarding his unselfish outreach to mentor and motivate young men to make better life choices. In 2010, he received the Montbello High School Annual Community of Champions Award for his Choice Program, a K-12 program for boys. Born in Houston, Texas, Mike has lived in Colorado since age eleven. He attended college at Grambling State University and Metro State College where he majored in music and minored in

Business and Accounting. Mike just completed his first book project.

Heidi Williams: Heidi Williams is a dual member of the Simply Speaking Toastmasters Club #677476 and Absolutely Articulate Toastmasters Club #1272692 both located in Aurora, Colorado. Heidi is the co-founder of Eleanor's Garden, LLC, a company that creatively makes portable garden beds. This aspiring entrepreneur attended Iowa State University, where she earned her Bachelor's degree in Landscape Architecture in 1989 and attended Golden Gate University where she earned her Masters of Business Administration in 1998. While attending Iowa State University, she proudly served on the Taekwondo NCTA Championship Team. Heidi is single, and when she is not working on her new Eleanor's Garden business, she enjoys time with friends and family.

Tyler Withrow: Tyler Withrow is a dual member of Gates to Excellence Toastmasters Club #3413 and Rocky Mountain Toastmasters #739. He has delivered forty-three prepared speeches during his three years in Toastmasters, and won Best Speaker for thirty-four of them. He has participated in eleven club contests, making it to the area level for six of them, and culminating in a second place finish at the District Finals for the 2010 Humorous Speech Contest. Tyler has worked at CoWest Insurance Associates, LLC for the past ten years and has grown to enjoy what is now his career. A voracious reader, Tyler absorbs a book a week and gives a detailed analysis of each to anyone who will listen. At twenty-nine years old, he lives a happy life with his happy dog, Max.

Frances Woolery-Jones: Frances is a member of Absolutely Articulate Toastmasters Club #1272692 located in Aurora, Colorado. She is a Christian woman and a Sunday School Teacher at the Potter's House of Denver, her home church. Frances is currently employed with the Cherry Creek Public School District as the Director of Special Education. Frances earned her BS degree in Elementary Education and a minor in Special Education from Culver-Stockton College in Canton, Missouri, and a MA degree in Education Administration from the University of Illinois in Springfield, Illinois. She is a native of Springfield, Illinois, and married to her husband for twenty-nine years; they have two children. Frances enjoys reading, singing, dancing, laughing, teaching children and serving others.

Diane Woods: Diane Woods is a member of the Aurorators Toastmasters #2136 Club. She learned to appreciate the power of language by teaching thirty-four years of secondary English. After she retired, she substituted in Aurora high schools for ten years. In addition, Ms. Woods has traveled overseas over thirty times, sometimes leading groups, and she has created an extensive landscape garden. Now she is a volunteer teacher for Osher Lifelong Learning Institute, a program for adults who want to keep on learning. In order to keep growing and challenging herself personally, Diane joined Toastmasters this year and looks forward to pursuing a journey of public speaking.

Shelley Xiao: Shelley Xiao is a member of the Solar Toastmasters Club #9548 located in Broomfield, Colorado. As a skilled and talented toastmaster, she has won club, area and division speech contests. In 2009, she was chosen as the target speaker for the district evaluation speech competition. Shelley was born, raised and educated in both China and the United States. Although she has mechanical engineering and business finance degrees and works as a senior financial analyst, she loves to write short stories and poems. Shelley hosted numerous musical shows in Shanghai's major theaters, and her first writing was published when she was in elementary school. Since age eleven, she has performed voice-overs for cartoons at Shanghai Animation Movie Producer; while in China, she also received awards for her theater stage plays. The talented and creative Shelley recently directed a Chinese New Year celebration show in Denver, Colorado.

Affiliations

Our co-authors are affiliated with the following District 26 Toastmaster International Clubs:

- Absolutely Articulate Toastmasters Club #1272692 (Aurora, Colorado)
- Aurorators Toastmasters Club #2136 (Aurora, Colorado)
- Castle Rock Toastmasters Club #3680 (Castle Rock, Colorado)
- Cherry Creek Toastmasters Club #2977 (Denver, Colorado)
- Defenders of Speech Toastmasters Club #897557 (Aurora, Colorado)
- Double Talk Toastmasters Club #4444 (Various Metro Denver, Colorado Locations)
- Eagle Valley Toastmasters Club #1464508 (Eagle, Colorado)
- Excelsior Advanced Toastmasters Club #3247 (Lakewood, Colorado)
- FACCMasters Toastmasters Club #5086 (Colorado Springs, Colorado)
- Gates to Excellence Toastmasters Club #3413 (Denver, Colorado)
- Meridian Mid-Day Toastmasters Club #7326 (Englewood, Colorado)
- Pioneer Toastmasters Club #2932
- (Lakewood, Colorado)
- Ranch Raconteurs Toastmasters Club #873616 (Highlands Ranch, Colorado)

- Rocky Mountain Toastmasters Club #739
  (Denver, Colorado)
- Simply Speaking Toastmasters Club #677476
  (Aurora, Colorado)
- Skyline Toastmasters Club #1038
  (Denver, Colorado)
- Speak Up Toastmasters Club #6015
  (Colorado Springs, Colorado)
- Solar Speak Toastmasters Club #9548
  (Broomfield, Colorado)
- Spirited Speakers Toastmasters Club #1440289
  (Centennial, Colorado)
- Summit Toastmasters Club #7064
  (Frisco, Colorado)
- Toastability Toastmasters Club #863184
  (Denver, Colorado)
- Wry Toast Toastmasters Club #8358
  (Greenwood Village, Colorado)

**For more information about
Toastmasters International, Inc.,
contact them directly at 949-858-8255, on
the web at www.toastmasters.org or via
US Postal Service at P. O. Box 9052,
Mission Viejo, California 92690 U.S.A.**

"On Being Happy"

I once wrote a song
That no one sang,
I once wrote a poem
That no one read,
I once painted a picture
That no one saw,

 And I wondered. . .
Why do I do these things?

Then one day
I sang my song
And I read my poem
And I saw my picture

And I knew why
And I was happy.

Author Unknown

CPSIA information can be obtained at www.ICGtesting.com
Printed in the USA
BVOW031514260911

272102BV00002B/2/P